When Greek Meets Greek

By G. H. Teed
(1886-1938)

First published in The Union Jack magazine,
Feb, 15th, 1913. No. 488, New Series (2nd).

Stillwoods Edition, 2019

Stillwoods.Blogspot.Ca

Catalogue Information:
Title: When Greek Meets Greek
Author: G. H. Teed (1886-1938)
First published in: The Union Jack. Feb, 15th, 1913. No. 488, New Series (2nd).
This Edition by: Stillwoods, 2019. (Doug Frizzle)
ISBN Canada: 978-1-988304-89-2
Blog: Stillwoods.Blogspot.Ca
Author Blog: http://ghteed.blogspot.com/
Storefront: http://www.lulu.com/spotlight/lulubook22

Keywords: Sexton Blake, British fictional detective, Mademoiselle Yvonne Cartier, Dr. Huxton Rymer

The Skipper desires to draw his readers' attention to the fact that "<u>When Greek Meets Greek</u>" has been written expressly for this issue of the Union Jack.

With is presented No. 2 of our wonderful soul-stirring new series of yarns which open to public view Sexton Blake's startling adventures, while opposed to that mistress of science—Yvonne.

These Yarns are confidently recommended for readers of <u>all</u> ages and of <u>either</u> sex! Every care has been taken to make them equally attractive to Old and Young alike, and the Skipper is satisfied that they really are so!

Synopsis: Dr. Huxton Rymer and Mademoiselle Yvonne Cartier join forces to steal bullion from Salvarita, Blake is on the case. Neither Blake nor Dr. Huxton Rymer know the real purpose of Yvonne—and certainly the President does not know why he is kidnapped!

Yvonne has her reasons—she will be deterred by no one!

Stillwoods Editions are a poor complement to some great stories and authors. Doug Frizzle is 'Stillwoods'; in retirement I needed something to do on 'foul weather' days.

First I found the author, A. Hyatt Verrill, from New Haven, Conn. He had been prolific and popular in his time but was forgotten even to Wikipedia. His books were difficult to locate—they were acquired from used book dealers as far away as Australia and South Africa. They were such great reading I began to republish them. I started with an autobiography of the author, unpublished, that I located at University of British Columbia—that Archive had no idea how they acquired it!

So I entered the publishing business. I am using Lulu.Com; it is a print on demand publisher so the costs are quite manageable. I spent 15 years on Verrill!

Then I found 'Luke Allan', a Canadian, namely, Lacey Amy, who wrote stories while he travelled the world, but they were mostly about 'Blue Pete' an American Half-breed who evades his enemies by going to Canada; Medicine Hat, Alberta, to be exact, and is befriended by a Mountie. Again these books were scarce, and no one knew this author was a Canadian. There are Stillwoods Editions of all of his 54 novels—two were published anonymously!

Lately, I've discovered New Brunswick's G. H. Teed, 1886-1938—prolific and forgotten. The vast majority of his 400+ novels were published anonymously and as 'pulp' novels. They were available weekly on England's newsstands and were very popular but as they were made of inferior paper, they deteriorated quickly. But over the years, English collectors speculated and researched these works, discovering a series of authors, and G. H. Teed was one of the greatest!

Teed's works were mystery and suspense—detective novels featuring 'Sexton Blake' or 'Nelson Lee' as cerebral sleuths with great physical training. As this 'About Stillwoods' is being created, one collector of Sexton Blake has provided me with some 200 scans of Teed novels. At this time I have re-published about 65 of his works as either blog posts, or the longer stories as Lulu imprints.

So that is the story on Stillwoods and myself, there are a few other authors and works I have added along in my journeys.

The quality of Stillwoods Editions is perhaps not great. I have no training in any of this digitizing and publishing business. I do not stop to make perfect products. I would rather have ten ones, than one ten!

I hope you enjoy these authors—their works are nearly a hundred years old!

Disclaimer: Each work may contain language and racial terms that is not appropriate to today. I apologize for them; I know that the author was using his voice to excite an adventurous English audience. Most every work has characters of redeeming ethnicity within.

I hope you enjoy and share these stories; I have.

Doug Frizzle

frizzle@hfx.eastlink.ca

About G. H. Teed

There are discrepancies in the reports on the history of G. H. Teed. This narrative is mine and may be more or less accurate.

George Heber Teed was born 1886 near Saint Stephen, New Brunswick, Canada. His father was a landowner and entrepreneur. He was educated in New Brunswick and then was sent to McGill University, where he probably graduated about 1907.

He had an itch for travel and for the Caribbean; once the travel bug got him he travelled far. He worked in Costa Rica and Australia before he travelled to England and began to write detective thrillers.

He was not great with money, he was very social and spent much time in taverns. Reports are that he was often in debt even though he was a prolific writer in popular magazines.

He took some time of in war service in the Great War.

He spent considerable time in France.

He also took a few years off around 1921, again getting the travel bug. These travels were around the world. These travels added authenticity to his stories, and his stories always had excellent plots and characters.

He died in 1938. Some of his works are listed as by G. Hamilton Teed—apparently he did not like Heber, so he adopted Hamilton as a familiar name.

Perhaps the best description of the man and his works is contained in the book '**Forgotten Authors Volume 3**' by Steve Holland.

Bottom of Suez
Crooks' Vendetta
Voodoo Island
Five in Fear
The Grey Ghost
The Case of the Duplicate Key
The Temple of Many Visions
Gangland's Decree
The Clue of the Four Wigs
The Mystery of the Film City
The Black Abbot
Murder Ship
Spies Ltd.
A Mystery of the Big Woods
The Mystery of the Kidnapped Killer
The Secret of the Swamp
The Case of the Pink Macaw
The Terror of Gold-digger Creek
The Case of the Mummified Hand
Pearls of Doom
The Victim of the Gang
The Case of the Courtlandt Jewels
Nelson Lee and the Lhassa Red Menace
The Riddle of the Russian Gold
Voodoo Vengeance
Hounded Down
Bribery and Corruption
The Sacred Sphere
The Tiger of Canton
The Crook of Marsden Manor
The Affair of the Six Ikons
The Secret of the Coconut Groves
The Case of the Disguised Apache

Under the Eagle's Wing
The Rogues' Republic
The Mitcham Murder Mystery
The Brotherhood of the Yellow Beetle
When Greek Meets Greek

See http://ghteed.blogspot.com/
For some of G. H. Teed's shorter works and articles about
this Canadian author.

PROLOGUE. I. Dr. Huxton Rymer Tries His Fate—His Success.

IF you know Puerto Costa, that dirty, smelling, sandy, fascinating tropical port, which boasts a really fine harbour, you will know the main street which runs at a distance parallel to the moon-shaped harbour, the proudest possession of the tiny republic of Salvarita.

If you know this street, you will know, if you have poked beneath the surface, the disreputable district which stretches between street and harbour, and if you have gone very deeply into the submerged life of the cosmopolitan port, you will also have more or less knowledge of those unspeakable dens of iniquity which fringe the harbour—their ever-open doors, throwing a constantly beckoning light to the newly-arrived sailor, and their dark, surrounding alleys forming a convenient spot into which the victim is tossed when its night-born vultures have finished with him.

In one of the lowest and filthiest of these dens, if there is any grade in them, sat a big, strong-jawed man. His seedy appearance created no desire in the many sinister, appraising eyes of the other occupants of the den.

He was silently cursed as a hated Gringo, but although his soft felt hat almost covered his face, his visible jaw created respect amongst the dusky horde, and he was left in peace.

For several nights running had the man occupied the same seat in the same den.

The first night of his arrival, a big negro had questioned his presence in no uncertain terms; but one piercing look of contempt from the intensely peculiar eyes of the Gringo had abashed the black, who slunk away with a sickly grin.

Since then he had been unmolested, which evidently suited his purpose.

Such was the appearance of Dr. Huxton Rymer on a certain night in Puerto Costa.

On this, the fifth night, he had ordered his drink of "white eye," that fiery, maddening drink of the native and the black, and had sat immovable as the motley, ever-changing crowd moved about him.

All nationalities were there, but the negro and the coast mongrel—mixture of Indian, Portugese, Spanish, black, and what not, predominated.

Idly they loafed from den to den, their bestial eyes seeking for an "honest man." Their quest was not for the same type of honest man for whom Diogenes searched, and they used no lantern to guide them. In their case an honest man represented one with money in his pocket, and brain-stealing "white eye" in his stomach.

Rymer sat unmoved throughout it all, his ears deaf to the quarrelling voices and the tinkle of a broken guitar, his eyes cast, apparently, into his half-filled glass.

But, though they knew it not, no man, negro, half-breed, or white, entered or departed than those all-seeing eyes did not search him absolutely with a glance of lightning rapidity.

For Dr. Huxton Rymer was decidedly "up against it." A little affair in New York had caused him to seek a more hospitable climate, especially after one Sexton Blake had arrived in the great American city.

Rymer, with his natural gift of "sangfroid," had taken the first steamer regardless of her destination. She happened to be bound for Salvarita, but not for the legal port of entry.

A large consignment of innocent-looking cases, marked "sewing machines" and "farming implements," had been landed at a solitary spot on the coast.

A sudden desire for agricultural pursuits seemed to seize a large portion of the populace, for they gathered at that lonely spot in large numbers, and eagerly seized upon the cases of ploughs, etc.

The shippers seemed to have made a sad mistake, for on being opened, the cases were found to contain many Mauser rifles and a large supply of cartridges.

But the peace-loving people had nobly swallowed their disappointment, and had shared the arms amongst themselves.

When the solitary passenger, Rymer, had seen their noble restraint in the face of disappointment, he had joined them.

Since they had guns, it seemed a pity not to use them. Consequently, a little shooting-party was organised, with the Government as the target, and, naturally, having shared their disappointment, Rymer had shared their deal.

Unfortunately, the shooting-party ended rather abruptly, for the Government had strenuously objected to being used as a target, and their reply had been very much to the point.

The noble-minded rifle-party had broken up in haste, and

consequent on this, Rymer, almost penniless, had drifted to the river dens, there to seek fresh pegs by which to again, ascend to the roof of luxury which he loved so well.

Not until two half-drunken Spaniards entered did Rymer move. As they sat at the next table, he shifted carelessly, but when he had resettled himself, his head was sunk in obviously drunken slumber upon his drink-stained chest, albeit his ear was in a straight line with the adjoining table.

The two Spaniards called in loud voices for drinks, and their following conversation was more picturesque than interesting.

Rymer was looking upon his elaborate movement as wasted time, when the conversation veered, to a topic which caused him to listen.

"So, Senor Alvarez, you will grace the president's ball with your presence to-morrow night?" remarked the elder of the two, a short, stout-bearded individual.

"Si, I go surely, I know none in the city but you, Senor Gomez, and I would meet some of the women for which it is famed."

"Caramba, you are sly dogs, you men from the haciendas! You have, then, a card?"

"Si. In my district, I am a strong supporter of the Government. I receive cards every year, but not for years have I been in Puerto Costa."

"Ha! Well, amigo, I trust you will enjoy it. For me, I am too old for such caperings. But come, we will make a night of it to-night. Let us go to the cards."

"Bueno!" grunted the younger, rising heavily.

Arm in arm they passed out of the door, but hardly had they been swallowed up in the sinister shadows before two of the villainous habitues of the den followed them. They, too, disappeared, and Rymer, stumbling to his feet, reeled out after them.

As the gloom enwrapped him, he dropped his staggering gait, and quickened his footsteps, closely dogging the pair ahead.

"It's a hundred to one chance," he muttered, "but you never can tell. Those two cut-throats had mischief in their eyes, and, who knows, something might fall my way, and, Heaven knows, I need it! Any way, it can't make things worse and in a week I'll be stony. Curse Sexton Blake. If ever I get him where I want him, Heaven help him!"

His eyes gleamed savagely in the darkness, and so absorbed was he that for a moment he did not notice that his quarry had disappeared. He hurried on, and coming to a dark, narrow lane, peered up. Far along hung a solitary red lantern, symbol of a gambling den, and against its dim reflection, Rymer could see several dark forms. Even as he looked, a smothered cry floated down to him, and the noise of a scuffle followed.

Drawing his revolver, and breaking into a run, Rymer dashed up the lane. As he had thought, the two mongrel negroes had left the den with the intention of attacking the two Spaniards, and had seized upon the dark lane as an opportune place.

The Spaniards were already on the ground when Rymer arrived, and the blacks were bending over them. The new-comer did not stand upon ceremony. Springing forward, and using the butt of his revolver, he struck with all his strength at one of the blacks.

The negro had turned and risen in alarm, and Rymer's blow caught him with crushing force between the eyes. He dropped, and none too soon, for his companion, with a snarl, had drawn a knife, and was coming for Rymer.

Rymer dared not shoot except as a last resort, for a shot would bring dozens of the human vultures on the scene, and he would stand small chance of getting clear. He acted quickly and silently. His left hand shot forward, and grasped the negro's wrist. Evading the negro's attempt to retaliate by doing the same with his free hand, Rymer again brought the butt of his revolver into play. Twice he struck before the blow affected that hard skull, but his second attempt achieved his purpose, and the negro dropped.

Sinking on his knees, Rymer opened the coat of the nearest Spaniard, A few moments' manipulation of the expert fingers sufficed to transfer the belongings of the unconscious man to himself. He could just make out the features of the man called Alvarez, and was turning his attention to his companion, when he heard footsteps approaching.

The police rarely ventured into that district, and when they did, it was in force and well armed. Their inspection was of the most cursory nature, and was made merely as a matter of form. This night had evidently been chosen for one of their mock inspections, for in the swinging lantern light, Rymer could make out the police uniforms on the men coming up the lane.

With a silent curse, he stole silently away, quickening his

footsteps as he turned down another black tunnel.

"Just my luck," he muttered; "but, anyway, I got something, and it may not be such a bad haul after all. Another five minutes, and I'd have cleaned out the other. It's a toss up if the police don't relieve him before they take the pair back to their hotel."

The police did take the pair back to the hotel, where they awoke the next morning sadder but wiser men, and the gay Senor Alvarez lost no time in taking the first train back to his hacienda, vowing that never again would he favour Puerto Costa with his presence.

Rymer held his revolver ready for action, as he hastily wended his way out of the black hole, but beyond one encounter with a negro whom he settled summarily, he reached his miserable lodgings in safety.

"By Jove!" he muttered, his eyes glittering as he emptied the contents of his pockets on the table, and looked them over by the feeble candle light. "A thousand pesos. Not much, but enough for a time—two rings, worth a hundred quid, anyway; watch and chain, not worth much; scarfpin, solitaire, must be worth forty pounds; and a handful of gold; and, what's this? Oh! Yes, the card to the president's ball!

"Huxton Rymer, my boy, I believe the wheel has turned at last. You are certainly in luck to-night, anyway. I wonder if I dare risk using this card to-morrow night. Yes, by Jove, I'll do it! When luck turns, follow it up. It's hard to tell what I might run into to-morrow night."

And with these pleasant reflections, Dr. Huxton Rymer sought his bed, and sank into an untroubled sleep.

TINKER WAS LIFTED UP AND A MOMENT LATER WAS FLUNG OVER THE RAIL.

RYMER FOUND HIMSELF GAZING INTO THE BARREL OF A REVOLVER.

BLAKE CAUGHT THE CHINAMAN IN A THROTTLING GRIP.

U. J.—489

II.   The Palace Ball—The Unbidden Guest.

THE small Republic of Salvarita, like many of her sisters, has seen many vicissitudes; but when this story opens, the little republic had completed her fifth year without any revolution of note, with the exception of the fiasco which Rymer had joined. Perhaps the reason of this was the firm hand, which controlled the course of events.

That hand belonged to one James Pearson, a foreigner, who had drifted into the republic five years previously.

The country had been torn by dissensions at the time of his arrival, and his keen, organising mind had seized the opportunity presented.

He had identified himself with the landed party, and six months later a vigorous policy had evolved a semblance of order out of the chaos which reigned.

Where he had come from no one knew, and his unheralded entry was forgotten in the reflected glory of his court—for President Pearson knew his people, and the exact value of a glittering spectacle with them. Consequently, the past five years had seen many gorgeous demonstrations, not least among which was the annual presidential ball, to which the leading lights of all parties were bidden.

Pockets were strained in order to ransack Paris and London for suitable gowns, and if they were twelve months behind the fashions of those centres, what mattered it?

To this glittering spectacle had the unfortunate Senor Alvarez received a card of invitation.

A prosperous coffee-planter, he rarely came to Puerto Costa, and, in fact, his present unfortunate journey was his first for some years.

And it was to this same spectacle that Dr. Huxton Rymer betook himself in his one remaining suit of evening clothes, with the card of the coffee-planter in his pocket.

All the best of Puerto Costa were there that night, and President Pearson, big and coarse, with heavy grey beard and iron-grey hair, received his guests with a pleasant smile, and a genial handshake.

The big ball-room at the palace was decorated with a mass of luxurious, trailing, tropical plants, their heavy odour ascending on all sides. Over the windows, and along the walls were draped flags of the republic, and at one end, framed in smaller flags, was a picture of the popular president.

The decorator had cunningly banked the thick green, so that many secluded tete-a-tete spots abounded in its shelter. For the present they were deserted, all the guests being in the thick of the entertainment in the main room; but afterwards, when supper was over, and hot, Southern heads were made hotter by wine; very few of the secluded nooks would remain unoccupied, and the heavy, twining plants would hear many flowery speeches of mercurial Spanish love.

The evening was well advanced, and the president had retired from the reception before Rymer risked an entrance into the thronged ball-room.

His knowledge of Spanish was passable, and a small, black moustache, with a military imperial; gave him a decidedly Spanish appearance.

He had passed the guards carelessly, the footman barely glancing at his card, and he presented a picture of distinguished nonchalance as he leaned against a bedecked pillar near the door.

His eyes roamed around the brilliant gathering with a bored expression, and little did any of that gay company think that the man who lounged so carelessly against the pillar was using an exceptionally clever brain to utilise some of them for his purposes.

After an hour's survey of the dancers, Rymer, with a barely concealed yawn, wandered aimlessly through the room, and sought the buffet.

The many green-banked aisles confused him for a moment as he entered their heavily-scented shelter, and he paused to turn and seek another way out.

He stood for a moment with a natural appreciation of the surrounding beauty, when something caught his eye which caused him to step softly back into the concealment of a spreading palm.

Through the heavy tangle in a neighbouring nook, he could just distinguish a slim, beautiful, bronze-haired girl.

She was alone, but it was not that which created such interest in the watching man's eyes. Rather, it was her occupation, and truly it seemed a strange proceeding even in that land of strange happenings.

In her hand was a delicate, jewelled, ivory-handled fan, which she held end up.

As Rymer watched, she pressed a spring in some invisible part, and the end of the round handle flew open. Into this the girl dropped a glittering diamond pendant and chain, and closed the top with an almost imperceptible click.

This done, she opened her fan, and languidly moving it to and fro, left the secluded spot, the while she hummed a lilting French chanson.

"Curious performance, my dear young lady!" murmured Rymer, as he also turned. "I'll just keep my eye on that little fan. What luck!" he chuckled. "Who would think that ivory handle contained a small fortune. She's probably frightened of losing it," he added to himself, as he once more entered the ball-room.

Rymer sought his old position against the pillar.

Not for a moment did his eyes leave the bronze-haired girl.

"She was evidently someone of consequence," he mused, for he noticed that the highest officials and the brilliantly uniformed officers struggled in friendly rivalry for the opportunity of dancing with her.

Supper was over, and the weary dancers had again scattered, when a loud gong brought them all with wondering eyes back to the ball-room.

An elderly Spaniard, evidently one of the high officials of the Government, held up his hand as the last couple returned.

"I regret to say," he began, in a loud voice, "that Senora Alfreda, the wife of our honoured Secretary of State, has lost her diamond pendant. It needs no description, for you are an familiar with it, the pendant being the one which the people of this republic presented to the senora in recognition of her services to the wounded during the trying times of five years ago when our beloved president came amongst us,

"It is inconceivable that anyone bidden here would retain the jewel if he found it, and I ask you as loyal Salvaritans if you find it to return it to the senora."

Loud exclamations of astonishment greeted the statement, and the guests looked nervously at one another.

A personal search of that fiery-natured crowd was out of the question, and the philosophic natures settled the matter off hand.

"If it was lost, it would be found and returned. If it had been stolen—well, it was a matter for the police, and it would teach the senora to guard more carefully the tokens of esteem presented to her by the people."

Half an hour later it had been forgotten by most of them as the evening went merrily on, but one among them was far from forgetting it.

That one was Dr. Huxton Rymer.

His lids had dropped to hide the exultant gleam in his eyes as the loss was announced, but not so much that he was unable to surreptitiously watch the face of the bronze-haired girl.

She stood beside a uniformed captain of cavalry, carelessly swinging the ivory-handled fan. Her attitude altered not a whit as the old official spoke, and her brows lifted with just the proper surprise. She turned with a smile to her companion as the music again started, and a moment later her small, blue-slippered feet were flying over the floor as though such a thing as a diamond pendant did not exist.

"By thunder," ejaculated the watching Rymer, with a look of intense admiration, "you're the coolest hand I've seen for a long time! Ye gods, what luck I'm in!" he chuckled. "My little, bronze-haired senorita, who would think you were so clever! Huxton Rymer, my boy, your star has certainly risen again.

"And now to introduce myself to my future partner, and future partner you are going to be, my child, although you don't know it yet!"

With self congratulation, Rymer sought the refreshment table, and fortified himself with the sparkling wine which flowed with reckless prodigality at the president's entertainments.

Had Rymer known the identity of the girl whom he proposed to make his future partner he might have gone ahead with perhaps a little less assurance.

Sexton Blake could have enlightened him, for in the bronze haired girl he would have recognised Mademoiselle Yvonne, the temper of whose steel he had tested.

"THE senorita looks tired. Perhaps she might care to rest in the quiet of the palms yonder?"

Mademoiselle Yvonne looked up, and her eyes narrowed a trifle as they met those of the man bending over her.

"I think you have made a mistake, sir!" she replied icily.

"Hardly," returned the man urbanely. "I must be rude enough to confess that, for the moment, your name has slipped my mind, a matter which is easily rectified by your own charming lips. But a mistake, no, senorita, don't be cruel enough to call it a mistake."

"Sir, you are insulting." responded Yvonne. "Leave me, or I will be compelled to call someone to my assistance."

"I don't think the senorita will do so," answered the man. "Pardon my presumption, what an exquisite article!"

Deftly he secured the ivory fan which lay in her lap, and before the angry girl could speak, he continued:

"Yes, it is truly an exquisite piece of work. Fifteenth century, is it not? I am a keen collector, senorita, so you will forgive my enthusiasm. Did you ever examine some of the old fans one can pick up in Venice? Really, they give quite an insight into the secretive natures of the old Venetians. Quite an education, I assure you. Most of them have the most fascinating secret springs, which send the end flying open, and, presto! we have a splendid hidden receptacle for secret letters, compromising papers, or even jewels. Now, if this is genuine, as it seems, I wouldn't be surprised if it also had a secret spring. Did you ever try to find out, senorita?" he asked, bending down with a smile.

"Who *are* you?" whispered Yvonne tensely.

"But, as I remarked before, senorita, you look tired. Won't you reconsider your cruel words, and rest for a little amongst the palms?" he inquired suavely, ignoring her question.

Yvonne was white with anger and mortification at the unknown man, but his appropriation of the fan had seemed significant. True, his words were coolly impersonal, but a dry glitter in those mocking eyes indicated a deeper meaning to the words.

Yvonne did not know the meaning of fear, and she was probably far superior in subtlety to the man who addressed her. But for the moment he had the advantage of her. In some way, he must have a knowledge of the contents of the ivory-handle of her fan. Was he detective, or was he thief? She did not know, and in humouring his desire to retire to the palms, she would move warily and endeavour to discover. Consequently, her words were tempered to her decision as she replied to the smiling question.

"Very well, senor," she smiled, rising. "I will adopt your suggestion, but first, my fan, please!"

"Presently, senorita—presently. Do not, I beg you, deprive me so soon of the pleasure of carrying it," answered Rymer, in a mocking tone.

Yvonne bit her lip, and allowed him to lead her to the seclusion of a palm-enclosed nook.

"Now, senorita," went on Rymer, bowing Yvonne into a seat, "we can talk in comfort. Perhaps you would prefer to rest in silence, or would you care to renew the discussion of ancient fans?"

"I will be glad if you will drop this trifling, and come to the point," said Yvonne coldly. "You sought me out apparently with a purpose, and I await some enlightenment."

"Certainly, if the senorita wishes; but as yet I have not the honour of the senorita's name."

"We will waive that formality for the present. Please proceed."

"Very well, senorita," replied Rymer, dropping into the seat beside her. "But first, permit me to tell you a very brief story."

"Keep to the point, please, and tell me why you sought me out."

"But my story contains the point," smiled Rymer.

Yvonne resigned herself to listen, and Rymer brought his eyes to bear on her as he began.

"Once there was a man, senorita, and he was very poor. Why, has nothing to do with the story. Unfortunately, he desired many things which he had been accustomed to, and which his poverty could not supply, him. He was very clever; and when he called himself clever, it was not from conceit, for only one man in the world had succeeded in getting the best of him, and that man is the cleverest detective in the world. But, senorita, the man's time will come, and when it does—" And Rymer finished, with a significant shrug of the shoulders.

"Ah!" interrupted Yvonne. "And has this detective a name?"

"Yes, senorita; we will give him a name, and although it is well known, you may not know it. We will call him Sexton Blake."

Rymer glanced down at the fan in his hand as he spoke, and did not see the expression in Yvonne's eyes as he mentioned the name.

"To continue," he went on. "As I said, this man was very clever, and consequently, when he found himself without money in a foreign country, he looked around for a chance to retrieve his fortunes. Fate led him to a brilliant reception one night, and while there he saw a beautiful young woman doing a most extraordinary thing. She stood behind a bower of palms— and, by the way, senorita, it wasn't unlike this one— and, lifting a beautiful ivory fan, she pressed a secret spring. The top flew open, and into the hollow of the handle, senorita, she dropped a beautiful diamond pendant. She closed the top and went back to the dancers.

"The man thought the beautiful young woman owned the gems, and was in fear of losing them. He watched her as she danced with the most prominent of the guests, and he was sure his deduction had been correct. As she seemed to have plenty of this world's goods, senorita, the poor man decided to relieve her of the fan and its contents, but before he found an opportunity a strange thing occurred.

"The wife of one of the most prominent guests lost a very valuable diamond pendant, and a search failed to reveal it. The man, senorita, immediately thought of the one he had seen the beautiful young woman drop into the handle of her fan. He listened to a conversation, and the description he heard tallied exactly with the one he had seen.

"Consequently, senorita, he changed his ideas about the beautiful young woman. Instead of taking the fan from her, he would join forces with her. Working together, what could they not achieve? Therefore, he sought out the young woman, and told her of his desire. What do you think her answer was, senorita?"

"Your story is very interesting, senor," replied Yvonne coldly, "but I really fail to see the point."

"This is the point! senorita," interrupted Rymer, pressing the secret spring, and catching the glittering gems which tumbled out. "You see," he continued, "the beautiful young woman was clever enough to secure the pendant, but, unfortunately, she failed to retain it. The poor man succeeded in getting it, but it was really a small thing compared with what they might have had if they had worked together, for doubtless the beautiful young woman belonged to one of the upper families, and could gain an entree wherever she desired."

"I must confess, senor," answered Yvonne, with blazing eyes, "that the point of your story is clearer. If she were an ordinary young woman, she might be tempted to permit the man to keep the gems, since he needed them so badly; but, being what she is, she will trouble him for them —quick!"

She spoke in a quiet voice of deadly calm, and Rymer looked up in amazement, to find himself gazing into the barrel of an extremely business-like-looking revolver.

"Quick!" repeated Yvonne, as he hesitated. "As you can see, my 'clever' friend, it is fitted with the latest silencer, and the sound doesn't carry a yard."

"Senorita," murmured Rymer, with barely concealed chagrin, passing over the stones, "I admired the young woman of my story, but I evidently rated her too low. I bow to superior odds, and much more than ever would I desire to work with the beautiful young woman."

"Listen, senor!" answered Yvonne, as she dropped the gems back into the handle and thrust the fan into the bosom of her gown. "I will tell you a story as well. Perhaps you will be cleverer at seeing the point than I was.

"Once there was a girl, and she went to a brilliant ball. She was not an ordinary girl, and she had not been long in the country. In fact, she had only arrived a few days previously, and was living aboard her yacht, which lay at anchor in the harbour."

"Ah!" ejaculated Rymer. "I can already see, senorita, that you are far superior at story-telling than I; but pray proceed."

"While at the ball she was watched by a man who, thinking to take advantage of what he saw, approached her, and made certain proposals. He foolishly imagined that she was a simple young thing, who had managed to find a diamond pendant. But it took her best abilities to secure that pendant, senor, and she meant to keep it. While the floor was crushed with dancers, she had reached forward and secured it, and her greatest skill had to be used in order to avoid discovery. So you can see, senor, she was hardly the type you thought her. In reality, she was something very different, as she proved to the man later. She led him on, to see just how far he would go, and when she was quite ready she demanded back her gems, and—she got them, senor. This man, senor, in his arrogance, kindly offered to take the young woman as his partner. The young woman, senor, shares her supreme power with none; but she took pity on the man, and decided to admit him to her confidence, and give him an equal share on certain conditions."

"I am interested to know the details," murmured Rymer.

"The details, senor, were that he should never question her authority. She needed a really clever associate; one to be equal to herself in all but final authority. You mentioned a very clever detective in your story, senor. Sexton Blake you called him. Well, my story also contains a detective, and, strange to relate, he has the same name. It might interest you to know, senor, that this detective was offered the same thing which the young woman of my story offered the man in the palm bower, but the detective preferred the other side of the fence. What do you think the man's answer would be, senor?"

"I would say, senorita." drawled Rymer, "that the man's answer would be 'yes,' with all the conditions agreed to."

"Shall I finish the story, senor?"

"Decidedly!"

"Very well. The man of the story accepted the woman's offer. She then invited him to her yacht in the harbour at ten o'clock the following morning. There she would discuss with him the details of the agreement, and outline to him a particularly big proposition which was being entered upon at the time, and in which he could share."

"I would say the man accepted the invitation with extreme pleasure," remarked Rymer. "But how did the man in the story know the young woman meant all she said?"

"He was not in the position to be able to choose but trust her," replied Yvonne coolly; "but if he doubted her word, he might consult the detective whom we previously mentioned. Sexton Blake is the young woman's enemy, but he would accept her bare word under any conditions."

"For once I think the man would do well to emulate the admirable detective," laughed Rymer. "He accepts her word, senorita."

"Very well, senor; and now your name, please?"

"Dr. Huxton Rymer, senorita. Ah, I am flattered! I see my poor fame has reached your ears."

"Yes, I have heard of you," replied Yvonne, studying him closely. "And now I am tired. Come to the yacht in the morning, and ask for Mademoiselle Yvonne," and she smiled maliciously as she saw the look of consternation on Rymer's face as he heard the name of the famous adventuress.

"Good heavens!" he muttered, as he followed her from the nook. "To think I took her for a simpleton. She certainly played with me to perfection. But, Huxton Rymer, my boy, you are certainly in luck. To-morrow—to-morrow, to begin again. And you, my charming partner, will lend a decided zest to the game."

IV.   Yvonne Grows Confidential—The Plan.

DR. HUXTON RYMER expended a large portion of his remaining funds early the next morning in a new outfit. He felt the occasion warranted the expenditure, and at five minutes to ten he entered a small boat at one of the wharves.

He was resplendent in new white ducks, white canvas shoes, and a broad, white helmet. Sticking from his pocket was the watch-fob belonging to the unfortunate Senor Alvarez. One of that gentleman's rings adorned Rymer's finger, and his scarfpin also did duty for the occasion; for to Rymer it mattered not from whence they came so that they did come.

He recklessly threw the negro boatman five times his fare, and ascended to the deck with a jaunty step.

Yvonne was reclining in a large wicker-chair on the shady side, and she presented a picture of dainty freshness in a yachting costume of white serge.

"You are punctual, my friend," she smiled, giving Rymer her hand. "Be seated. You sent your boat back?"

"I did, mademoiselle," smiled Rymer, in reply.

"That was right," answered Yvonne. "We will talk alone until lunch, and then I will introduce you to my uncle and the other members of the circle."

"That will suit me admirably," rejoined Rymer. "May I smoke a cigar while we talk, mademoiselle?"

"Certainly," laughed Yvonne. "I will join you with a cigarette." And she lifted a tiny silver reticule as she spoke.

Rymer lit his cigar, and settled himself to listen to her words. The sailors were working on the lower deck, and as far as he could see they were quite alone where they sat.

The sky was a deep blue, and the blinding glare of the overhead sun was broken by a cool canvas awning. The atmosphere was pleasantly languid, and Rymer's blood coursed, in pleasant anticipation as he cast an appraising eye at the white paint and shining brass of what he hoped was to be his future home for some time. For luxury abounded on every side, and luxury was the chief aim of Rymer's life. Not for him the smaller but honest rewards earned by the sweat of the brow. Others could have that, but he—he would take advantage of the present opportunity, and this time he would achieve the permanent reward of brains, which until now, Sexton Blake had always snatched from his grasp.

Yvonne spoke slowly and clearly, and the blue wisp from her cigarette ascended into the still air.

"Have you an intimate knowledge of Salvarita, Mr. Rymer?"

"No, not intimate, mademoiselle I only landed here a few weeks ago. But I know every foot of Puerto Costa, and also the coast-line for some miles. You see," he added, with a grin, "I landed here unheralded; but, unlike the popular president, I joined the wrong side."

"Ah! Yes, I remember reading of the sudden ending of the revolution a short time back. You know something of President Pearson, then, do you?"

"Only what I picked up here," he replied;

"Do you know anything of the inside of the Government?"

"Yes, naturally," he replied. "Monero, who came over to the rebels, was in the Government, and he told me a lot. It was inside news that influenced me to join them."

"What was the inside news, might I ask?"

"Only a matter of a loan which the Government is negotiating in London for a matter of two millions. It would have been very pleasant, to have a share in the expenditure of that loan, and as it is based on the customs receipts for fifty years, it wouldn't matter to the lenders who was in power, for the agreement provides that they shall place their own man in charge of the customs."

"I see you do know something of their plans," remarked Yvonne, "for your information about the loan is quite correct. But what would you say if I told you that you might yet share in that two millions?"

"I would say it is too good to be true," answered Rymer, his eyes lighting at the thought.

"It may be; but, at any rate, we are going to have a try for it."

"Good heavens!" ejaculated Rymer, sitting up. "Is that a fact?"

"I never state anything else!" said Yvonne drily.

"And is that the big thing you spoke of last night in which you said you wished me to join?"

"Exactly," smiled Yvonne, lighting another tiny cigarette.

"Then, mademoiselle," he cried, "you can count Dr. Huxton Rymer very much into it."

"That is settled, then," remarked Yvonne. "And now I will give you the details.

"You perhaps don't know that the loan has been definitely arranged for the first of next month?"

"No, I didn't know that."

"Well, it has. But you, of course, know that the new Government bank which our friend Pearson is building is still unfinished?"

Rymer nodded.

"Well, I have it on most excellent authority that the two millions will be shipped from London in bullion by special steamer. It will arrive here between the fifteenth and the seventeenth. I also have it on excellent authority that until the bank is finished, the whole amount will be placed in the president's palace for safe keeping. A guard of ten men will stand over it night and day, and the work on the bank's vault will be rushed forward in order to receive it. For extra safety, it will be stored in the room adjoining the president's bed-room.

"That, my friend, is the situation, and you can rest assured it is correct in every detail. Now, for the rest of it. That two millions is all in gold bullion, you understand. It will arrive safely, and will be stored safely. But I have decided that we can find a much better use for that two millions than the Government of Salvarita. I hate to deprive those worthy ministers of the chance of feathering their nests for life; but, my friend, we are going to get that bullion."

"Good heavens," gasped Rymer, "it is so enormous it seems almost too big to try for! But, by thunder, what a scheme!"

"Wait, you have not heard all," continued Yvonne. "It is big— yes, but we have unlimited funds to draw on, for— pardon me for the remark—I seem to have been a bit more successful than you. We also have plenty of willing hands, for every man on this yacht shares pro rata in the circle. For that reason, it is not too big for us, and my plans have been most carefully thought out. No trail will be left by me, and I trust you have done nothing by which you can be traced."

"No, I assure you nothing," answered Rymer.

"That is well, and now for the rest. In addition to the bullion, we are going to take their president as well. Suspicion will naturally fall on him, and the search will be for him, not us. I have a place in the South Sea Islands to which we will take the bullion and the president. I might inform you that the securing of the president is as important to me as the bullion. For the money alone, I would not bother at the present time, but I have a personal score to settle with President

Pearson."

"It is magnificent, magnificent. Mademoiselle, I bow to you. It will be a pleasure to work with one whose ideas are so stupendous, and who has the brains and money to carry them out. Is it a strictly personal affair you have with the president?"

"Yes, and that remains my secret. It is of old standing, and I have watched him for years. My chance has now come, and I will take it. More than that, it is not necessary for you to know. We will get under weigh to-morrow, and cruise about until the arrival of the bullion. My uncle is the treasurer of the circle, and you can draw on him freely for any amount you need. I might say that at the meeting of the circle this afternoon you will be elected vice-president, and I trust you will be loyal to the circle."

"Mademoiselle, I am deeply grateful for your offer, and I swear to you I will be absolutely loyal to the circle."

"And now I will leave you," she said wearily. "I am tired, and desire to rest before lunch. Enjoy yourself here until the gong goes, and then I will introduce you to your future associates over whom you will have direction."

Rymer rose as Yvonne departed, and when she had disappeared down the companion-way, he sank back in his comfortable chair, and dreamed pleasant dreams until the luncheon gong sounded.

Below, in her state-room, Yvonne lay face down on the small brass bed which she had had placed in her cabin.

Her eyes were closed, and her lips moved in a whisper.

"On—on, always on. But I have taken up the plough, and must follow it to the end of the furrow."

She rose as the gong sounded, and the smiling, clear-eyed Yvonne, who entered the luxurious saloon, was radically different from the weary girl who had lain face down on her bed a few moments previously.

None of the circle knew of the weariness of Yvonne's solitary hours. They only knew the iron-willed, dominating girl, who directed them and led them with marvellous success, and to only one man had it ever been given to know her in any other way. That man was Sexton Blake.

.   .   .   .

The next day the beautiful white yacht sailed gracefully out of the harbour of Puerto Costa, and dipped her dainty nose into the blue

rollers of the Atlantic.
    END OF PROLOGUE.

THE STORY.

THE FIRST CHAPTER.   Arrival of the Bullion —Yvonne and Rymer Take a Hand—The Capture.

PRESIDENT PEARSON, although he wore outwardly his usual stern expression, was in a jubilant frame of mind.

He sat before his desk in the executive-room at the palace, and sighed with satisfaction as he signed and sealed with the arms of the republic the last document before him, and passed it to the waiting secretary.

"Just hand this to the agent in charge of the bullion, Cortez," he said, turning to his secretary, "and pass the word to the guards to be in readiness to escort it up from the wharves."

The Spanish secretary hastened away to do his bidding, and as the door closed, the president leaned back in his chair and lit a cigar, he permitted his features to relax as he puffed contentedly at the mellow Havana, and his lips moved, his murmured words indicating his train of thought.

"Not so bad, by thunder! Two millions, and I need it. The army hasn't been paid for six months, and the guns are terribly out of date. A little railway up to Santa Rosa, and that land of mine will be worth a handsome figure. A good reserve for the new bank to work on, and I'll clear up a fortune out of that."

And truly President Pearson had cause for self-congratulation. Five years previously he had landed in Salvarita, penniless and unknown. The revolution which was in progress had turned the wheel of fortune for him. He had joined the landed party, and threw himself heart and soul into the campaign. The timely death of the general commanding had made it necessary to elect another. By pulling the proper strings, and by sheer force of character, Pearson had secured the vacancy.

More than ever did he vigorously prosecute the campaign, and on the victory of his troops, the presidential chair had been a natural step for him. The army stood by him to a man, and if the chief office had not been offered to him he would have again taken the field. Whence he came, none of his confreres knew, but had inquiries been made throughout the mining districts of Australia his identity could soon have been established.

An unfortunate occurrence in Melbourne in which he had been mixed up had caused his sudden departure from that city, and

Salvarita had been chosen as his destination, not so much on account of its climate, as the fact that no extradition laws existed.

Consequently, considering the conditions of his arrival, Fate had certainly used him kindly.

As yet he had remained unmarried, but his intimate friend and partner, General Mendoza, the Salvaritan Minister in London, had a charming daughter, and rumour said that the senorita would soon become the president's wife. General Mendoza was the wealthiest of the Salvaritans, his fortune being estimated at something like five millions. His daughter was his only child, and Pearson had a comfortable sensation in the region of his heart when he thought of the inevitable journey of that fortune on the general's death. In the meantime, the general was to settle a round million on the senorita when her marriage took place.

President Pearson's thoughts broke off, and his face assumed its wonted sternness as the door was opened by the returning secretary.

"Everything is arranged, sir," he said.

"Captain Alameda is taking ten of your bodyguard to escort the bullion to the palace. They will remain on guard until midnight, when Lieutenant Sandra, with ten more of your guard, will relieve him. They are placing it in the room next to your bedchamber, sir, and I have sent word to Lieutenant Sandra to keep his men quiet during the night in order not to disturb you."

"Very well, Cortez. Thank you," replied the president. "Did you find out what progress is being made on the vault at the bank?"

"Yes, sir. The contractor hopes to have it ready for use by the end of the week."

"Very good. I am calling a Cabinet meeting this evening, Cortez, to ratify my proposals about the increase of pay to the army and the payment of all back allowances. I will be glad if you will notify the members, and meet me at the council chamber at eight."

The president had a highly successful meeting that evening. Substantial increases were voted for the army, and an order was passed authorising the treasurer to pay all back allowances. The president's proposal to spend a good sum for new weapons was received with enthusiasm, for he had taken care to have a majority of the military in his Cabinet. Other expenditures were tentatively discussed, and as the president rose he was greeted by long and enthusiastic cheers.

He received their ovation with smiling dignity, and sought his chamber next that which contained the bullion; but he stopped to have a word with Captain Alameda, and to glance with satisfaction at the valuable cases which would make things so wonderfully pleasant.

He dropped a discreet hint as to the resolutions of the evening, for it would be well to have the information disseminated through the army as soon as possible, and he had no doubt as to the rapid spread of such welcome tidings.

He passed on to his bed-room, and retired. A hard day had made him tired, and before the guard changed at midnight, the president lay in a deep slumber.

•　　　•　　　•　　　•　　　•

While things were running so smoothly at the palace this evening, other events were happening at a lonely spot on the coast some fifteen miles away.

A rakish, white yacht, with all lights doused, steamed slowly up and down a short mile from the white, sandy beach.

As eight bells struck, several dark figures emerged from below.

They hastened to the davits, and at a signal from the captain lowered away two large flat rafts, on each of which reposed a long, roomy motor-car.

Slowly and carefully they worked until the rafts reached the water, when they stood waiting further commands.

Yvonne appeared from below, followed by Rymer and Graves— her uncle.

"It's fortunate the sea is so smooth," remarked Yvonne, "otherwise we would have been compelled to utilise the wharf at Boro, a few miles along, and that would be more risky,"

"Yes, things seem to be working well," answered Rymer, as he puffed at a cigar. "I suppose we'd better be getting along now, hadn't we? You say the guard is to change at twelve, and we will need to have a good look around before going ahead with the plan."

"Yes, we'll start now," answered Yvonne. "You take one lot, and I'll take the other. My uncle can go with you, and Hendricks with me. Captain Vaughan will remain in charge of the yacht. That will give you seven men, counting yourself, while I will have six. Three to remain with the captain will be sufficient."

A few minutes later the two rafts were being propelled towards the shore, and in half an hour they grounded gently on the sloping beach.

No time was lost in getting the cars ashore, and the men, filing silently into the cars with all lights out, headed at a moderate pace for Puerto Costa, Yvonne driving one, and Rymer the other.

It was eleven o'clock when they reached the town, and Rymer took the lead as they entered its environs, heading by a little used road, until he pulled up in a thick wood in the rear of the palace.

The palace stood practically alone on a high hill, and for their purpose the lack of surrounding buildings suited them well.

Silently the two parties descended, and leaving one man to guard both cars, struck across through the woods in the wake of Rymer.

A few minutes' walk brought them to a deserted spot on the main road leading from the palace to the town, and here they dropped silently to the ground.

The silence was broken a little later by the rattle of vehicles, in which the members of the Cabinet were returning to the town; but as the sound of their wheels died away in the distance, silence again reigned for some time.

It still lacked a few minutes of midnight before anything else occurred to disturb the quiet of the night.

The regular sound of marching feet came up the dark road, and not until then did the silent watchers stir.

Swiftly and silently did Rymer arrange his men.

Half he sent across into the deep shadow of the other side of the road with whispered instructions.

"Ten to one they'll be marching in pairs. Pick your man, and use your sandbag before he can cry out."

They had barely assumed their positions when the marching footsteps grew close, and as the little band appeared, they stopped in stupefied amazement as several dark figures leaped at them from each side of the road. Their surprise had been calculated upon by Rymer and Yvonne, and before a cry could be uttered the sailors were at work with their sandbags. It was over in a moment, and Rymer congratulated himself on its swiftness and lack of outcry.

"Hurry!" he whispered. "Put on their coats, belts, and caps, and take their rifles. Your own dark trousers will pass. Then bind them and gag them with the things we brought."

He himself appropriated the coat and sword of the lieutenant in charge, and so quickly had the operations been carried out that it still wanted a minute to midnight as the uniformed party entered the palace gates, Yvonne and her uncle following at a short distance in the rear.

Two men were on guard at the gate, but before they could cry out they shared the fate of the others. The clock over the palace just started to boom the hour of midnight when Rymer and his men entered the main door and ascended the staircase.

Down the passage they went, and the subdued clink of arms in a neighbouring room told them the guards still on duty were preparing for their release.

Rymer knocked at the door with the handle of his sword, and as it opened his eyes gleamed with satisfaction on seeing the dim lights. That fact meant, perhaps, ten seconds of advantage, and in the present position those ten seconds would be of immense value.

Captain Alameda, who opened the door, looked surprised as Rymer and his men entered.

"Why," he said, lifting his brows, "I expected Lieutenant Sandra. Why hasn't—"

But the captain got no further. With a lightning spring, Rymer was upon him, and before the astonished captain could cry out, Rymer's fingers had closed on his throat.

The mock guard had taken their cue from Rymer, and each picking his man, leaped for him.

The hardy sailors were used to a rough and tumble fight, and knowing things would go hard with them, if the alarm were raised, they wasted no time in preliminaries.

As quickly as one guard was overcome, he was bound and gagged, and Yvonne barely reached the room when the panting men straightened up, the last guard secured.

Captain Alameda lay senseless on the floor where Rymer had thrown him. One of the sailors bound him, and thrust his own handkerchief in between his teeth, and the job was done.

"You have done well, my friend," whispered Yvonne to Rymer. "And now let us lose no time in securing the president."

The scuffle had not been without noise, but President Pearson was a sound sleeper, and still lay in slumber as Rymer, with three men, softly opened the door of the bed-chamber and entered.

A small nightlight was burning, and the outline of the president's form was visible under the coverlet of the great four-poster bed.

With a panther-like tread Rymer crossed the room, and the president awakened from his golden dreams a moment later to find four men in the uniform of his own guard bending over him.

He started to sit up but found himself securely held, and as he opened his mouth to give the alarm, a silk handkerchief choked the sound.

Silently he was lifted out, and his clothes put on him.

His eyes glared in blazing anger at his captors, but he had no choice but to submit. He made an attempt to struggle, but a sudden twist of his arm reduced him to quietness.

His clothes on, the three dusky sailors hoisted him up, and followed Rymer out.

Rapidly, they carried him to where the motors were, and returned to help their comrades in removing the bullion.

The last box had been placed in the car, and still the palace lay wrapt in the unknowing slumber when the engines were started and the cars headed for the sandy beach fifteen miles away.

SEXTON BLAKE apparently found something of interest in the morning paper, for he replaced his cup in his saucer, and devoted both hands to holding the sheet.

Twice he read the article which had caught his eye.

"Here, Tinker," he remarked to the lad who sat opposite him at the breakfast-table, "read this article, and tell me what conclusions you come to."

He passed the paper across, his finger pointing to the paragraph, and with a thoughtful look proceeded with his breakfast, while Tinker read the article which stared at him in bold outlines:

"EXTRAORDINARY SITUATION IN SALVARITA! PRESIDENT PEARSON DISAPPEARS! TWO MILLION POUNDS IN GOLD BULLION ALSO DISAPPEAR! GREAT EXCITEMENT IN PUERTO COSTA! MARTIAL LAW PROCLAIMED! THE ARMY IN A FERMENT!

"Cables have been received describing an extraordinary state of affairs in the Republic of Salvarita.

"President Pearson, who has been the chief executive for five years, has mysteriously disappeared, leaving no trace.

"Two million pounds in gold bullion has also disappeared with him. This large amount had just been landed from England, and was a loan arranged with Messrs. Crick, Field & Co., the well-known London banking firm.

"The Opposition accuse the missing president of decamping with the bullion, and demand the immediate resignation of the Cabinet.

"The army still believe in foul play, and the finding of the palace guards bound and gagged lends weight to their argument.

"The Opposition, however, insist that it is part of an elaborate plan.

"In the meantime, the army controls the situation, but matters are reaching a critical stage.

"An interesting point is that just before his disappearance, President Pearson carried several proposals involving large expenditures for the benefit of the army. This fact probably accounts for the attitude assumed by them.

"President Pearson was shortly to be married to Senorita

Mendoza, daughter of the wealthy Salvaritan Minister to London.

"Further developments will be anxiously awaited."

(Later.)

"Further details are at hand regarding the disappearance of President Pearson.

"A fisherman states that in the early hours of the morning he saw two boats leave the beach about fifteen miles from Puerto Costa, and proceed to a yacht, which was cruising about with all lights out.

"The Opposition point to this as evidence of President Pearson's guilt, and the army, after holding out for some time, have given in.

"The Cabinet has resigned, and Senor Martina, the leader of the Opposition, is temporarily at the head of the Government.

"Our representative called upon Senor Mendoza at the Salvaritan Embassy, but was unable to obtain an interview.

"Messrs. Crick, Field & Co. have as yet no further information than ourselves."

"Looks as though the president had made a pretty clean 'get away' with the bullion, guv'nor," remarked Tinker, as he finished reading.

"I see you agree with the article that he is guilty," laughed Blake.

"Why, yes," responded Tinker. "Don't you, guv'nor?"

"Well, looking at it casually it would seem so," replied Blake; "but let us look into it. We have a few minutes to spare, and the matter interests me, for you will remember it was in Puerto Costa that I ran Barnes, the big forger, to earth."

"Oh, yes; I remember, guv'nor. Then you know Puerto Costa."

"Quite intimately," laughed Blake, rising and entering the consulting-room.

"Now, Tinker," he continued, walking over to the bookcase, "I will just refresh my memory by referring to my Index. Ah, here it is!" he exclaimed, turning to the letter "S."

" 'Salvarita—South America. Population 700,000.' Then follows a long string of figures relating to the customs, receipts, foreign debt, etc. 'Capital, Puerto Costa, has a fine harbour. Form of government—Republic, governed by a president and legislative council. President: President Pearson, who is also commander-in-chief of the army.' There are a lot of notes quite beside the question," said Blake, skipping a paragraph. "All, here we are again.

" 'Unknown generally from where President Pearson came.

Arrived in Salvarita five years ago. Rumoured engagement to Senorita Mendoza, daughter of Salvaritan Minister to London.'

"That is all," he remarked. "Now we will turn to "M." Here it is:

" 'Mendoza, Jose. Salvaritan Minister to London. Extensively interested in plantations, etc. Rated by Braddun at five millions. Age about 60. Has one daughter, aged 25, his wife being dead.' "

Blake closed the Index, and, returning it to the shelf, walked over to the window.

"Well, guv'nor, what do you think of it?" asked Tinker, "Doesn't it look as though the president was guilty?"

"It looks that way. Tinker," answered Blake; "and it is possible it was intended to look that way. But it has points of very great interest. I would like to know what Senor Mendoza— Why, hallo! Isn't that— yes, it is Senor Mendoza coming up the steps!" jerked out Blake, returning to his seat. "He looks in a dickens of a hurry, and if I'm not mistaken, we'll hear more of this case."

Blake lit his black pipe, and stretched himself out in his chair. Hardly had he done so when Senor Mendoza was announced.

He was a small, dark-skinned man. His hair and moustache were grey, and his dark eyes were filled with worry.

"Come in, Senor Mendoza," smiled Blake. "I see you are quite convinced of his innocence, and believe in the theory of foul play. I don't know but what I agree with you."

"What—how?" gasped his visitor, sinking into a chair. "I don't understand, Mr. Blake. How did you know I came about President Pearson, and that I believe in his innocence?"

"Very simple," laughed Blake. "President Pearson in his five years of office has undoubtedly acquired a fair amount of property in Salvarita. Then he becomes engaged to your daughter. She is your only child, and will eventually get all your fortune, which is in the neighbourhood of five millions. President Pearson mysteriously disappears, and with him two million bullion.

"Had he anything to gain by doing that, when he would have control of the spending of it in any case? Would he leave a place where he ruled with almost absolute power, and was honoured and respected, to go into hiding when it was not necessary?

"He had more to gain by remaining.

"Then you come to me in a state of great agitation, senor. If you believed in his guilt, you would have stirred up the police in every capital in Europe, unless the Government has already done so. But the fact that you come to me at all proves you believe in his innocence and wish to find him."

"Extraordinary!" gasped the Minister, his mouth agape with astonishment. "Mr. Blake, they have not overrated you. I have come for your assistance, for I know it is impossible for him to be guilty; but alas! besides myself and my daughter who is prostrated, I am afraid no one else believes him guiltless."

"Suppose you tell me a little more," suggested Blake.

"Very well; I will. What I know, but what no one else knows, is that Pearson owned lands alone in Salvarita which will be shortly worth as much as two millions. They are held in my name, and he was not generally known as being interested in them. In addition, I had promised to settle a million on my daughter on her marriage, and he knew they would get at my death the balance of what I had.

"That is why I know he is guiltless, Mr. Blake. My idea is that some of his enemies have done this, and that he is held a prisoner in the mountains of Salvarita. But your statement makes my explanation much easier than I thought it would be, and I beg of you, Mr. Blake, to take the case and find the missing man.

"Unlimited funds will be placed at your disposal, and needless to say, I will pay anything to have his innocence established, for, as I said, my daughter is prostrated, and I would pay any price to bring smiles back to her eyes. Will you take it, Mr. Blake?" he ended, looking anxiously at the detective.

Blake smoked in deep thought for some moments. Finally, rousing himself, he said:

"Yes, Senor Mendoza, I will take the case. It interests me on account of several features. I will start at once."

"Oh, thank you, Mr. Blake!" answered the Minister, springing to his feet and almost throwing his arms, in his effusive Spanish way, around the detective's neck.

"Don't spare money; all you need is at your disposal. In anticipation of your acceptance, Mr. Blake, I have hired Lord Cardby's yacht for an unlimited period. I thought if you accepted the case you might wish to leave for Salvarita at once. But in any event she will have steam up constantly awaiting your orders."

"Ah, that will be very satisfactory!" replied Blake. "I may decide to leave at once for Salvarita, and can make faster time than by the ordinary route. But one word, Senor Mendoza. Not a word to anyone—not even to your daughter—that I am working on the case. Let her think, if necessary, that I have refused it. If President Pearson does happen to be innocent, as we think, it points to a great force behind the affair, and you can see the necessity for strict secrecy if I am to work to advantage."

"Certainly—certainly, Mr. Blake; anything you say I will do. And you can trust me to keep the secret, for that is one thing at least in which we diplomats excel."

"Very well, that's settled, then!" rejoined Blake, rising. "I will communicate with you at intervals—if not personally, by my assistant."

And he indicated Tinker.

"Good! And now I'll be getting back. I wish you every success, Mr. Blake, for my beloved child's happiness depends on it."

Blake bowed, and a moment later the street door slammed behind the anxious little Spaniard.

THE THIRD CHAPTER.   Alone in Mid-Ocean—Tinker's Peril.

"WHAT do you think of it, guv'nor?" asked Tinker, when some time had passed.

"It would be futile to form any theory yet," answered Blake, rousing himself. "Of one thing I feel convinced, and that is that President Pearson did not disappear of his own free will. Naturally, many theories present themselves, and I may start on several false tracks; but they must be followed until they lead somewhere, or bring up against a blank wall. But now to business, my lad!"

Blake walked to the window again, and gazed out. Something caused him to suddenly withdraw behind the shelter of the curtain, and he peered cautiously through its thick web.

"We'll postpone arrangements for a bit, Tinker," he softly said, backing away. "There is a man on the other side of the street whose elaborately careless attitude makes me think this house is the object of his attention, for it is the only one at which he is not looking. It is just possible that he has followed Senor Mendoza here, and it may have something to do with the object of his visit. I am going to walk along in the direction of Oxford Street. Wait a few moments, and then follow. If he shadows me, keep him in sight, and see where he goes, for I will shake him off, if possible."

"Right, guv'nor, I will," answered Tinker, creeping cautiously to the window, and peering out. "He'll be easy to follow, for that light coat of his will be visible in any crowd."

"Don't depend too much on that," replied Blake, as he put on his hat and picked up his stick. "You yourself have often had on a light coat which you have rapidly changed to a dark one in the space of a few seconds, and our friend outside may possibly know that wrinkle."

"All right, guv'nor; I'll be careful," answered Tinker. Blake, closing the street door, stood on the step, and carelessly lit a cigar before starting out. The utter indifference of manner of the man across the street convinced the detective that he was being watched, and he glanced from the corner of his eye as he strode down Baker Street.

He swung around a corner, and hailed a taxi, and the appearance of his man, who also hailed a taxi, proved the truth of his suspicions.

Blake directed the driver to go to Oxford Street, and, on reaching that crowded thoroughfare, he pulled up before one of its large emporiums.

"Here, cabby," said Blake, tossing the man half a sovereign; "wait on the rank for about ten minutes and then drive away! Be sure and wait at least ten minutes."

"Right, sir!" answered the driver.

And as Blake entered the big store he saw the following taxi pull into the kerb.

He hastened through the building, and out at the back. Hailing another taxi he drove to Cockspur Street, and the absence of any following cab told him the ruse had worked.

"I hope Tinker won't lose him," he remarked to himself, stepping from the cab. "It's just possible, though, that he may spot the lad."

Blake crossed the footpath and entered the office of a steamship company. He emerged a little later, and in his pocket was a ticket for the Republic of Salvarita on a steamer sailing the following day.

He returned to Baker Street, and awaited Tinker's return, early afternoon had come before the lad came back.

"Well, did you find out anything?" asked Blake.

"No, guv'nor," answered Tinker ruefully. "I'm sorry, too, but he must have spotted me. I followed him until I saw you enter the store in Oxford Street. He went in after you, but came out a little later frowning, and I knew he had lost you. He jumped in his cab, and I followed in mine. I don't know just when he knew I was following, but I saw he had spotted me when his taxi started driving up one street and down another in an aimless fashion. Well, we finally got into the Strand. A block in the traffic stopped me, but he got through, and before I could jump out to follow he was gone."

"Never mind, Tinker," replied Blake kindly. "He was probably a shrewd fellow, and if I succeeded in shaking him off, it is no discredit to you to have been shaken off by him. But the events of this morning have caused a change in my plans. I am entrusting you, my lad, with one of the most important matters which has come under my hands, for I am going to send you alone to Salvarita."

"Jiminy, guv'nor! It's jolly decent of you to trust me so much. I realise the importance of the president of a country disappearing, and I promise you I will use all my endeavours to follow your instructions."

"I know you will, my lad. But let me impress upon you one very important thing. Watch yourself and everyone about you day and night. I am quite convinced that the man who gave us the slip this morning had followed Senor Mendoza, and that an attempt will be made to watch every move we make, for they will know as a matter of course that he came to see me in order to get me to take the case. It stands to reason that there must be a particularly daring band at work, and that they will spare no efforts to counteract any move we make."

"I'll remember, guv'nor," rejoined Tinker earnestly. "When do I start for Salvarita?"

"To-morrow morning," answered Blake. "While you and your unknown friend were playing hide-and-seek this morning I slipped down to Cockspur Street and got your ticket. The Orinoco sails at ten, but it will be wise for you to go aboard to-night. And now for your instructions."

Blake filled his old black pipe, and Tinker settled himself to listen carefully to his instructions.

Inwardly the lad was filled with pride, for Blake was showing great confidence in him to entrust him with such a weighty mission,

"You will go to Salvarita," began Blake, sending forth clouds of smoke, "and present a letter I will give you to Senor Martina, who is now at the head of the Government. He, being the leader of the Opposition, will naturally believe in the president's guilt, but that needn't bother you, for he won't have any idea of your mission. In fact, no one must know. But I did a bit of a favour for Senor Martina a few years ago, and he was more grateful than perhaps the occasion warranted. Consequently, he will do everything in his power to make things pleasant for you, and that is what I want.

"Puerto Costa will naturally be in a very excited state, and it will be difficult to get about freely. An authority from him will assist you to do so.

"Now, from the facts at hand, the case presents two lines of thought which we must follow. Firstly, has President Pearson been seized by native Salvaritans and taken prisoner to the mountains, as Senor Mendoza thinks, or, secondly, has the attack come from an outside source?

"If the second theory is correct, the yacht which the fishermen saw will be found to have played an important part, for the shipping reports show no vessels of any description have left Salvarita for five days.

"Of course, a third hypothesis, based on the theory of hidden facts yet to be discovered, may show both lines of thought to be incorrect, and that President Pearson is guilty.

"It would need a very strong hidden motive to make him take such a step, but I will be able to weigh this point more clearly when I have traced his life previous to his arrival in Salvarita.

"That is the case as it stands now. You will endeavour to find out all you can, and pay particular attention to the yacht which the fisherman saw."

"Yes, guv'nor, I will," answered Tinker earnestly. "But how about you? Aren't you going to take it up yourself yet?"

"I'm going to see how you make out," laughed Blake, in a non-committal manner. "I'll take a hand when the time arrives. I see you looking at Pedro," he continued, holding out his hand to the big hound. "Well, he's to remain with me for the present. You will be playing a lone hand, my lad," he added seriously, "and perhaps I am wrong to send you on such a mission alone; but the events of the morning have made it absolutely necessary."

"Oh, I'll be all right, guv'nor! I'll watch out carefully. What identity shall I take?"

"Well, I think the same as on your last trip to New York. Travel as a young man of leisure. You will, of course, have unlimited funds to support it. Communicate with me here at all times, but in case anything should happen that I shall have to leave suddenly, I will leave a sealed letter with full details with Senor Mendoza. He will deliver it on presentation of our code, a copy of which I will give him so that it won't fall into strange hands. And now, we have a lot to do before this evening, when I will give you final details."

. . . . .

The Orinoco was berthed at Tilbury, and Tinker went aboard at ten that night, as Blake had suggested. He had taken elaborate precautions to avoid being followed, and, for safety's sake, had parted from Blake at Baker Street.

He sought his berth early, resolving to keep to his cabin until the steamer sailed, and as he crawled into his bunk flattered himself he had got aboard unobserved.

The average steamer is usually held up for some time after her advertised time of sailing by the tag end of the freight, but the Orinoco slipped her moorings on time.

Tinker did not come on deck until they had reached the Channel. He spent the day sizing up his fellow-passengers, who were few in number at this time of the year, and all one class, for the Orinoco was a small steamer, and passenger traffic to Salvarita was light, even in the best season.

An elderly planter and his family, a young Spanish lady and her duenna, two lads about Tinker's age, going out as pupils on a coffee estate, a middle-aged, hatchet-faced woman, who looked as though she might be going on a solitary expedition to the wildest part of the Andes, but who in reality was a mild-natured missionary, and a husky-looking clergyman made up the party.

Tinker rapidly made friends with the two lads, and the captain and officers, seeming a very decent lot, Tinker looked forward to an enjoyable trip.

The second day the lads were busy organising sports to while away the time. Land dropped away from sight, and by evening they had settled down like old acquaintances.

A cold, driving rain came on during the evening, and those who had not gone below from sea-sickness sought the saloon's genial warmth.

Tinker found the atmosphere stifling, and, slipping down to his state-room, got his macintosh and cap.

He ascended to the deserted deck, and moved to the wet side, for he liked walking with the driving rain in his face.

He had been the sole occupant of the deck for some time, when he saw the big clergyman make his appearance.

The reverend gentleman stopped as he reached Tinker, and, swinging about, kept pace with the lad.

"Rather a dirty night," he remarked, as they walked towards the stern. "I see you, like myself, are fond of the rain."

"Yes, I am very fond of it," answered Tinker. "It clears the cobwebs away!" he laughed.

They had reached the stern, and were turning to go back as he finished speaking.

Suddenly, without warning, the big clergyman swung on him with blazing eyes. Springing for the lad, his huge hands closed on Tinker's throat.

"Oh, you do like the rain—eh? It clears the cobwebs—eh? Well, Mr. Sexton Blake's assistant, since you like water so much, we'll see if the ocean clears your brain, for into it you are going pretty quick!"

Tinker struggled fiercely in his assailant's grip, and once almost twisted free, but those huge hands held him with a deadly hold.

He reproached himself deeply at that moment for not being more careful; but really there was some excuse, for the so-called clergyman had conducted prayers with a most sanctimonious air. But Tinker realised with horror that the man's eyes were filled with a deadly purpose. It was not a question of avoiding being followed, but a fierce struggle for life itself.

His hands sought a grip on the man's body, but his antagonist was too powerful for the lad, and his brain whirled with despair as he felt his lungs bursting under that awful, choking pressure.

Everything swam before his eyes, his mind reeled. He gave one last, despairing struggle. His arms dropped, coming into contact with something. Tinker grasped it, to use it as a buffer between him and the man, but he was too far gone. Again his arms dropped. He felt himself being lifted up, and a moment later, still clutching his useless weapon, he sailed over the rail and sank with a splash into the cold, black depths, while the steamer ploughed her way through the dark, stormy night.

THE FOURTH CHAPTER.   Pedro's Warning.

HARDLY had Tinker left Baker Street to go aboard the Orinoco on his ill-fated journey when Blake hastened to his room and rang the bell.

Telling the landlady, who appeared in answer, to pack his bags, he returned to his desk and wrote many letters.

It was after midnight before he finished, but he had yet much to do.

A telephone message brought the big grey car around, and half an hour later, with Pedro and his bags in the tonneau, he threw in the clutch and headed for Plymouth.

Night still lingered over the water when he brought the car to a stop at the docks.

Around the harbour were dotted the lights of vessels at anchor, but it was impossible to make out any particular shape in the gloom.

Blake was turning to re-enter the car and await the coming dawn, when an early boatman passed.

"Good-morning sir!" he remarked cheerfully. "We'll have rain before another twenty-four hours."

"Good-morning! Do you think so?" replied Blake.

"Yes, sir. It's almost certain. Be you waiting for friends, sir?"

"No," answered Blake. "By the way, I wonder if you know where Lord Cardby's yacht—the Corsair—is lying?"

"Oh, yes, sir! She lays where you see those twin lights off yonder. Be you wanting to go out to her?"

"Yes. Do you want the job?"

"Certainly, sir. I'll have the boat ready in two minutes."

Blake sent the car back to London with the man, and entered the small boat.

Dawn was just breaking as he climbed the ladder to the deck of the beautiful yacht which had made a name for her speed.

A word sent one of the watch to notify the captain, who happened to be on the bridge.

"Come up, sir!" he called down to Blake. "I presume you are Mr. Blake?" he said, as Blake gained the bridge. "I hardly expected you so soon, but if you want to get away I'm all ready. By the way, my name is Pentland."

"Thanks, captain; I do, if you can manage it," replied Blake.

The captain was a slim, pointed-beard man of the Naval College class, and Blake could not help but admire the finished manner in which he issued his orders and secured their carrying out.

"Now, Mr. Blake," he said crisply, as the throb of the propeller sounded, "Mr. Ross, the chief officer, is relieving me in a few minutes, and if you care to remain up here until then, I will show you your apartments myself."

"Thanks, captain," answered Blake, lighting a cigar; "I'll do so. It will be a relief to get some of this beautiful morning air after London, although I got a good dose coming down."

"You didn't come by train?" inquired the captain.

"No; I motored down."

The yacht swung round as Blake spoke, and the morning sun, appearing above the horizon at the same time, shone with golden splendour on her gleaming brass.

Mr. Ross, the chief officer, appeared as the yacht got under way, and Blake liked him at once.

He was a young, smooth-shaven man, with keen eyes, and greeted Blake warmly as his eyes lighted with pleased admiration, for he had heard much of the famous detective.

He took the bridge, and Captain Pentland conducted Blake to his apartments.

They proved to be a sitting-room and huge sleeping-cabin, stretching clear across the after part of the yacht.

"I hope you'll be comfortable, Mr. Blake," said the captain, throwing open the doors. "I'll have a steward detailed to look after you, and if there is anything lacking, don't hesitate to ask. The whole yacht is under your orders, and if you tell me to go to the South Pole, I'll attempt it."

"I won't ask that, captain," laughed Blake; "but I'm glad to know I can depend on you. I can see I am going to enjoy my trip with you immensely. If you will send my steward to me I'll be obliged. And I will ask you to excuse me from appearing to-day, for I am dead fagged, and will sleep."

"Right, Mr. Blake! I'll do so."

Blake began wearily to undress as the captain departed, and the steward spreading out his pyjamas, the worn-out detective was soon fast asleep.

Perhaps he would have dropped into one of his concentrated

moods instead of seeking his bed had he known that barely had the yacht left the harbour when a throbbing motor pulled up, and the driver gleaned from a loitering boatman the fact that he had only a short time before taken a gentleman out to the white yacht which was disappearing in the distance. Much more would Blake have kept awake, and probably his instructions, which had been to sail for Salvarita, would have been altered had he seen the motor turn and proceed to a cable office, where a message was despatched to that chaotic republic.

But he did not know these things, and consequently he appeared at dinner that night, refreshed from his sleep.

He found the captain and Mr. Ross all he thought them. The chief engineer, Mackay, was a crusty Scotsman, with the heart of a lion, and the captain raised his brows in astonishment as the usually taciturn man thawed perceptibly under Blake's magnetic manner.

On the second night the driving rain, prophesied by the old boatman, duly set in, and the quartet gathered in the luxurious saloon for a game of bridge, the first of many to be on that voyage, which was to toss them all over the globe, and lead them through many perils before they again saw England.

Blake and the engineer were partners, and the detective, who found little opportunity for relaxation, threw himself completely into the spirit of the game.

How different would he have felt, and how his heart would have tightened, had he known that out on that black waste of waters Tinker, who was so much in his lonely life, lay struggling for life against the monstrous waves which were fast overcoming him.

Pedro, who had accompanied Blake, and lay under the table, raised his head at that moment, and all four men started nervously as the great hound emitted a deep baying wail.

The superstitious Scotsman raised his eyes nervously,

"I'm thinkin' soom mon has this moment gone to his death," he said solemnly.

A weird feeling came over the detective as Pedro got up and placed his head on Blake's knee, looking at his master with great pleading eyes, which seemed almost to burst in their endeavour to make the man understand.

"What is it, old chap?" said Blake in a reassuring voice. "You're not getting nervous of the sea after all these years of travelling, are you?"

But Pedro was not to be comforted. He paced restlessly about the saloon, finally casting himself down at the door, where he lay gazing into nothingness, with his great eyes wide.

The four men proceeded with the game, but the spirit had gone out of it after Pedro's strange wail, and they broke up early.

Blake called the dog as he went below, but although the faithful fellow pounded his tail in acknowledgment, he did not get up, and all Blake's coaxing failed for once to make him rise.

THE FIFTH CHAPTER.   The Stabbing of Sexton Blake.

BLAKE, with the exception of the one evening when Pedro had acted so strangely, enjoyed his trip immensely.

As he had expected, he found the captain and officers most congenial companions, and before the yacht arrived at Salvarita there was not a man on board, from the captain to the cook's boy, who would not go through anything for the detective.

In addition, the voyage benefited him greatly, for the previous months had been very hard ones, and little rest or recreation had entered his busy life.

But although Blake enjoyed his rare opportunities for relaxation, his active mind was not content for long to only puzzle over bridge problems, and consequently, when Captain Pentland remarked that another twenty-four hours would show the coast of Salvarita, Blake once more put everything from his mind but the business he had come on. Typical of his brilliant mental system was the complete manner in which he remarshalled all the points of the case, as though they had all been tagged and laid away for a few days.

He held a consultation with the captain that evening, and it was decided that the yacht should cruise about until nightfall the following day. Then she would draw closer to the shore, and a small boat would land Blake at a lonely spot on the coast. The yacht would then put to sea, and return a week later. A small boat would be sent ashore again at the same lonely spot, and if Blake desired to come aboard he would be there. If not, she was to put to sea again, and return in three days, when he would in any event be at the rendezvous.

This plan was put into operation, and the following night Blake, who had garbed himself as a dilapidated sailor from the wardrobe of the yacht, landed on the sloping beach of a small cove, and was soon lost to view of the returning boat in the dense tropical growth lining the shore.

According to the captain's chart, it was about seven miles from Puerto Costa, and as Blake gained the road he set out at a brisk walk for the town.

He was unaware that the appearance of the Corsair had been closely looked for, and that a stealthy figure dodged along the silent road behind him.

Had he taken Pedro, the hound would have scented the following man at once, but for the time being the faithful fellow had been left aboard the yacht.

On reaching the town Blake took himself to the disreputable district in the lower part.

He had been twelve days at sea, and although the Corsair was equipped with wireless, and they had picked up messages from passing steamers, nothing had been received referring to the situation in Salvarita, and consequently Blake was not aware of the latest developments.

That the country was still in a very excited and unsettled condition he quickly saw on reaching the town, and as he approached the water-front, the signs of disorder were more accentuated.

The whole underworld of that, at any period, evil district, seemed to be about.

The narrow streets, lined with the gambling and drinking dens, threw an extra stream of light into the murky surroundings.

The harbour was dotted with vessels, and the roaring, drunken songs, bellowed forth in every language, indicated the fact that the crews were on shore-leave.

All the side-streets were in darkness, their narrow blackness leading to mysterious retreats, and secure in their shelter, sinister figures—negroes, half-castes, and the riff-raff of the port—lurked and watched for their prey.

The motley cosmopolitan parties of sailors in every stage of drunkenness, reeled, and staggered from one noisy den to another, greeting with maudlin familiarity the drink-sodden habitues of the dens.

Woe to any who passed alone from den to den, or got separated from his companions, for the watching vultures in human form made short work of their prey.

Were he very drunk, a brawny negro, seized him in a choking grip, and before his muddied wits could seize on what was happening, he was hustled up a dark alley. A crack on the head sent him to the ground like a log, and a dexterous hand relieved him of his possessions.

But whether drunk or sober, the new arrival took his life in his hands when he entered those sinister tunnels, and no man possesses a record of the "reported missing" who never returned.

And it was into this abyss of crime and loathsome evil that Blake ventured.

He knew his way about the underworld of Puerto Costa, for he had passed through its darkest spots some years ago in his chase for the famous forger Barnes.

He saw things had not altered for the better since his previous acquaintance with it, and, in fact, as he got deeper he found that several new dens had started, and were apparently doing a profitable trade, to judge from the sounds of ribald merriment that came through the doors.

Cautiously Blake picked his way along. He had a definite object in view, for he passed many of the brightly lit places, and headed towards the darkest part of the district.

He made his way to a dark, uninhabited-looking building, and knocked in a peculiar manner upon the door, repeating it twice at intervals.

Some moments passed before a cautious whisper in Portuguese descended from somewhere above.

"Who knocks?"

"One who desires an audience!" replied Blake.

"Do you bring the pass-word?"

"Yes. Of the upper grade!"

"Name it."

"Todos!" whispered Blake.

"A moment, and I will admit you!" and a faint, shuffling sound came, followed by the cautious opening of the door.

When Blake had been in Puerto Costa before, he had, as mentioned previously, been the means of saving Senor Martina, the present head of the Government, from an extremely compromising position.

His movements at the time had led him into strange perils, one of which had forced him to take part in a terrible riot in the underworld. A quick shot had saved the life of the man fighting next to him, and the latter's gratitude had known no bounds. He had presented Blake with a beautiful emerald, and had conducted the detective to one of the strangest places he had yet been in. Blake had discovered the man he had saved to be as strange as the surroundings.

He was a wizened native, who was the head of a secret society. The old man had boundless wealth, drawn, Blake suspected, from some hidden mine in the interior. He ruled like a potentate, and although the outside of his den was dilapidated, the inside was in the most luxurious style imaginable.

Blake had been made an honorary member of the society, and this fact had been of great advantage to him previously.

Consequently he had sought out the old man this time, for he knew he would know every occurrence which took place in that mysterious underworld.

His guide led him along a dark, evil-smelling passage, and down a flight of steps.

Pausing, he knocked in the same manner as had Blake, and an invisible door swung open.

A flood of light gushed out, and Blake's eyes rapidly took in the scene, which looked exactly the same as it had five years previously.

The walls were hung with rich silks from China, a rare Turkish carpet that would have delighted the heart of a connoisseur, covered the floor—in the centre stretched a magnificently-carved table with attendant, comfortable leather chairs for the members. Huge copper lamps lighted the room, their brilliancy dying away in the silken folds on the walls.

But incongruous as did the room look for such a place, even more so as regards the room did the wizened, dark-skinned figure appear, who sat on a raised dais at the further end. His parchment-like countenance looked more like that of a Chinaman than a South American Indian, and Blake had often suspected that such was really the case.

He was dressed in a flowing yellow robe, and was smoking a "hubble-bubble" pipe. His eyes were deep-set and were the most remarkable feature in his face—all the wisdom and mystery of the ages seeming to congregate in those ancient orbs.

Blake bowed as he entered, but a wave of the hand motioned him to a seat at the foot of the dais.

"It is long since you were here," remarked the old man, in a soft, melodious voice.

"Five years, Giver of Light!"

"You have done well since then," continued the old man whom Blake had called by the grandiloquent name of "Giver of Light."

"You have had great success, and the good wishes of the 'Source' have been with you."

"You have followed my doings?" asked Blake, in a surprised

tone.

"Naturally," replied the old man. "I broke all precedent when I admitted you to the Source without knowing more about you, but I felt you were worthy. My confidence has been doubly repaid, for I have followed with satisfaction all your doings. But you have come for something. Shall I tell you what?"

"If you can," smiled Blake.

"You have come about the missing president."

"Quite right!" answered Blake, knowing his admission was perfectly safe. "And I have come to you, O Giver of Light, to ask you in your great wisdom a question."

"What is it? If I can I will answer."

"My reasoning tells me he is not in Salvarita," went on Blake. "Am I right?"

"You are. He is not in Salvarita!"

"Can you give me any further information?"

"That I cannot, and for a certain reason. I am in a hard position, my son. Only this can I tell you. Great and powerful interests are against you, and members of the Source themselves are in it. Between you, I must, by the rules, remain neutral. I regret that I cannot help you more, but I tell you, my son, give it up. The odds against you are too big, and—you will never find your man!"

"I am sorry," answered Blake, rising. "I quite see your position, and thank you. As to the odds and not finding my man, that remains to be seen," he added grimly. "And now, with your permission, O Giver of Light, I will retire, for I have much to do."

"Peace go with you!" answered the old man, returning to his pipe.

Blake was disappointed at the result of his interview. He had counted on getting valuable information from the old man, and knew from his words that he was fully aware of all the details of the president's disappearance.

"Well!" he muttered, buttoning up his sailor's jacket, which he had opened when in the room. "I've made a certainty of one thing, and that is, the importance of the other side. I'll have to take a shot at some of the dens, and find out something about the yacht if I can."

Blake started down a black side-street in the direction from whence he had come. As he passed an even darker alley, he heard the lapping of the water, and was changing his course in the direction of the water's edge to reach the dens more quickly, when that dark, silent figure which had followed him ever since he landed, seized his opportunity.

Blake had his hand on his revolver, and looked about him warily as he walked; but it was intensely dark in that locality, and, although he could not see another being, he knew that all around him sinister eyes were watching his progress.

These vultures he was on guard against, but not until too late did he hear the stealthy steps behind him.

He swung round quickly, and struck out fiercely in the dark, but he was too late, for the assailant lunged heavily, the long blade of his knife sinking deep between the detective's shoulders.

Blake's arm dropped, and with an almost imperceptible moan, he fell unconscious, his life's blood ebbing rapidly.

His assailant made off silently, not stopping until he reached a cable-office far up in the town.

Then he filled in a form, and a few minutes later the following words were speeding over the wires to London.

"Orinoco completed. B. finished to-night. All clear. Report to headquarters and advise any other instructions here."

THE SIXTH CHAPTER.   Yvonne's Revenge—President Pearson's Fate.

TO return to Yvonne and her associates who had put Salvarita in such a predicament.

The old fisherman had been quite right when he said he had seen two boats put off to a yacht which was cruising with all lights doused.

The captors of President Pearson had arrived at the beach safely, and had lost no time in transhipping their captive and the bullion to the yacht.

Yvonne gave orders to proceed to sea at once, and barely had the captured president been conducted to the cabin which was to be his prison, than the Fleur-de-Lys, her lights once more burning, put to sea.

She laid her course towards the south, and about the time Tinker met his fate in mid-ocean, and Pedro displayed his uneasiness on the Corsair, the Fleur-de-Lys was forging along at a rapid pace towards the Straits of Magellan.

A stop was made at Valparaiso, where Yvonne received a cable which had been forwarded from London, and which read as follows:

"Orinoco completed. B. finished. All clear. Report to headquarters and advise any other instructions here."

Her eyes filled with an intense weariness as she tossed it to Graves, who read it with satisfaction.

"Ah, that's good news!" he remarked. "We have been fortunate in our choice of agents. I can breathe more freely now with Sexton Blake and that assistant of his out of the way."

"I am sorry it was necessary," replied Yvonne; "but Sexton Blake seemed fated to cross our path, and since he refused to join us—well, he had to go."

But she rose as she spoke, and descended to her cabin, and certainly her associates would have marvelled had they seen her cast herself on her small brass bed and burst into a passion of weeping.

But none knew of the interview she had once had with Blake, in which he had refused the offer of her hand, and although she felt positive the old proverb relating to a "woman scorned" fitted her case, she realised since receiving the report of his death that her feelings had never altered.

Rymer was equally as elated as Graves on hearing of the end of

Sexton Blake and his spirits went up considerably.

"At last," he thought, "I will be able to achieve something. That cursed Blake won't be stepping in again to spoil my game, and lay me by the heels!"

President Pearson had been kept in close confinement since leaving Salvarita, but as beautiful, wicked Valparaiso dropped away behind, he was brought on deck previous to an interview with Yvonne, for she felt that now was the time for her triumph.

After dinner that night she dismissed all from the saloon, and sank into a chair awaiting the arrival of the prisoner. He came a few moments later, and glanced in amazement at the beautiful woman in the faultless evening-gown.

"So it's you, mademoiselle, to whom I owe my thanks for this unexpected hospitality. When you came to Salvarita with letters of introduction, which I see now must have been forged, I did not know in receiving you at my palace that I was nursing a viper, as it were."

The president had spoken in slow, measured tones, attempting to remain dignified in his galling situation; but he started visibly as Yvonne replied.

"As to whether I am a viper or not, we will let that pass," answered Yvonne, coolly lighting a cigarette. "But as to my hospitality, I am afraid you will have to put up with it for some time, Mr. James Pearson, one-time manager and director of the Jig Saw Mine in Australia, and one-time defrauder of innocent women!"

"What do you mean?" gasped Pearson, paling. "Who are you?"

"You may well ask," returned Yvonne. "If your former partner, Mr. Vineburg, alias Bechstein, were alive, he might be able to tell you; but as he isn't, I will condescend to inform you. My name is Carrier. Perhaps that will enlighten you somewhat."

"The daughter of John Carrier?"

"The same. I see your memory is quite good."

"But—but why have you abducted me and ruined me?" he asked dazedly.

"Do you need to ask?" answered Yvonne coldly. "Is it nothing that you and your associates swindled my mother and myself, first out of the mine, and not content with that, out of our home? It is nothing that the shock of your schemes killed my mother, and sent me into the world a penniless and friendless girl? Have you forgotten my vow to be revenged on you and your companions?" she asked bitterly. "That vow I have kept. Yes, you were very clever, you and your 'honest' companions! You took good care to keep within the law in your swindles on two helpless women, and you thought my threat of revenge was the idle ravings of a grief-stricken girl. Well, you have seen whether that is so.

"Your friend, Vineburg, alias Bechstein, has met his fate. I ruined him, and his suicide followed. You were the next on the list, James Pearson, and I have already accomplished your ruin. Every paper in the world is ringing with the tale of the absconding of former President Pearson, of Salvarita, with two millions of the country's money!"

"My heavens!" gasped Pearson, sinking into a chair, and mopping his brow in an agony of suffering. "Have you done that?"

"I have saved several papers, and will give them to you to read. You can see for yourself that I have done it. It might also interest you to know that Sexton Blake, your only hope, was sent in search of you. Well, that hope is gone, for he has been stabbed in Puerto Costa."

"Will you never be satisfied?" asked Pearson bitterly. "I ask no favour from your hands for myself. It would be a waste of time to tell you that I was never in sympathy with the deception practised on your mother. But is your nature so hardened with revenge that all womanly feeling has died?

"I ask you to consider Senorita Mendoza, my affianced wife. Keep the bullion, strip me of my honour, and send me into the world a broken man if you will; but I ask you to spare her. A line from you assuring her of my innocence in this affair. I assure you I changed my life, and threw off old companions, and have worked hard to build up the prosperity and honour which I achieved. Isn't that sufficient revenge for you? Will you have pity on the senorita, who has never harmed you?"

"Did you and your associates have pity on my mother, who never harmed you, but, on the contrary, as she thought, befriended you? Did you have pity on me when you forced me into the world to punish where the law wouldn't reach? Oh I have suffered, don't make any mistake about that!

"What has my life been since then? To achieve my purpose, I was compelled to build up a machine—a well-organised circle—and now even if I would release you I couldn't. Since the members of that machine have stood by me, they must have their reward. You it was, you and your companions, who forced me outside the law, and I have no doubt you will gloat when you know that the one being on earth I cared for, the man who started to search for you, was against me, and I have been compelled to agree to his removal.

"But that additional suffering will react on you and the rest of your associates, James Pearson, for it will increase the spirit of my revenge. Everything have you deprived me of, and as I have sworn, so will I do.

"As for the Senorita Mendoza, I will think it over. I have no desire to send a woman through the suffering through which I have gone. Now leave me. I will let you know my decision."

Pearson seemed to age under the lash of her tongue, and on being dismissed, he stumbled from the saloon, almost tottering from the realisation that he was a ruined, broken man.

Yvonne sat in deep thought after he had departed, and her eyes were filled with an aching sorrow. With a heavy sigh she rose and approached the exquisite mahogany desk, stopping before a long mirror on the way.

Long and earnestly she looked at her reflection.

"Yes, I am beautiful," she muttered. "I could have been a devoted wife to some good man. My brains would have assisted him to a high position. Instead, I am sent into the world, an adventuress. Forced to live a life I hate, and receive only the admiration of men whom, in other conditions, I would not wipe my feet on. Had things been different, even Sexton Blake, cold as he is, might have thawed. And then they ask pity."

She turned wearily away, and sat down at the desk. Picking up a pen she wrote, her hand travelling slowly over the paper.

Only a few lines, and the note had neither beginning nor ending. She read it over, and the text was as follows:

"Senorita Mendoza is informed that the missing president, whom the writer understands is the affianced husband of the senorita, is guiltless of the charge of absconding. But the senorita is further informed that he is receiving just punishment for actions of his earlier life. He is unworthy of the senorita's love, and she would do well to forget him. The senorita is warned that if this note is made public, it will be immediately known, and the president will meet with a swift fate. The writer has no desire to injure an innocent woman, and writes, in answer to the president's plea, in order to ease the senorita's mind."

Yvonne seemed satisfied with the contents, and, folding it up, she addressed it.

Typical was it of her nature that she refused to give Pearson any definite answer on the matter, but her yielding had its own reward in the mitigated suffering of the grief-stricken senorita.

BLAKE BOWED AS HE ENTERED.

THE WOMAN DREW BACK IN FRIGHT - AS A HUGE HOUND DASHED IN FOLLOWED BY TWO MEN.

BLAKE'S ARM DROPPED, AND WITH A MOAN, HE FELL UNCONSCIOUS

U. J.—688

THE SEVENTH CHAPTER.   The Spanish Woman—Her Reward—Blake Resumes the Battle.

WHEN Blake had dropped to the ground in the dark street where he had been stabbed, it will be remembered that he had immediately sunk into unconsciousness.

When he came to himself he was lying on a mattress in the corner of a dim, rickety room.

He tried to raise himself, but sank back in surprise on finding his muscles refused to support his effort.

His eyes grew puzzled in an endeavour to elucidate the reason of his being where he was. He was laboriously piecing together the events leading up to his departure from the house of the Secret Society, when the door opened and a woman entered.

She hastened over to the corner on seeing the detective's eyes open, and as she bent down, Blake saw the shattered remains of a once dusky beauty.

"The senor is better," she said, in soft Spanish. "I am glad."

"Where am I?" asked Blake weakly.

"You are safe, senor, and will now, soon be better. You were stabbed, and once I thought you were dead; but the senor is blessed with a wonderful constitution, and the wound is now nearly healed."

"Ah! I remember!" answered Blake, the memory of his attack returning to him. "But you say it is nearly healed. Have I been here, then, some little time?"

"Over ten days, senor, and always your mind was a blank."

"Over ten days!" echoed Blake, in amazement. "Then —" And he broke off, in anxious thought, as he remembered his arrangement to meet the yacht at the latest at the end of the ten days.

"What day is this, then, senorita?" he asked.

"Wednesday, senor. I brought you here on a Monday." Blake knit his brows in worried calculations. Two days since he should have been at the meeting-place. What would they think? Where was the yacht? What was Tinker doing? And what was the situation? All these thoughts chased rapidly through his mind, but he could find no solution to them.

"The senor must not worry," said the woman, speaking again.

"I am perplexed, senorita," answered Blake, gazing up into her dark eyes. "But I evidently owe my life to you and your care, senorita.
54

I wish to express my gratitude."

"No, no, senor! Don't!" she replied tensely. "If you knew all you would not thank me!"

"How do you mean?" asked the puzzled Blake.

"Oh, senor," she said, turning away her eyes, her dusky face turning yet darker with a flood of shame, "you owe nothing to me. I saw you leave the house of the society, and followed you to take advantage of you. A man reached you first, senor, but he left you without taking the contents of your pockets.

"I picked you up and dragged you in here, to take what you had and let you die; but I couldn't, senor. I know not why. Bad—terribly bad—have I been, and many men have been sent penniless from this place, but I could not bring myself to let you die. I dressed your wound, and— and I got interested in my work, senor. All your belongings are safe. See!" she said, rising and going to a small chest of drawers. "Only a few pesos have I taken, and that was to get things, for you. Not a penny have I touched for myself, senor."

"I quite understand, senorita," replied the amazed Blake, gently. "I owe you my life, and am deeply grateful to you. That it has in some way changed you I am glad, and your reward will be my care."

"I don't want a reward which you will give, senor," she said, in a low tone. "Of money I have enough. But you have talked too much, and must rest. Have you any friends? Can I—"

She broke off, and started up as a sudden noise came from without, and, as a deep bay followed, she sprang to the door, snatching up a revolver as she did so.

Blake raised himself, with a new-found strength, as he heard the sound.

"Don't shoot, senorita!" he exclaimed. "Open the door. It is my friends."

The woman lowered her arm and pulled open the door, drawing back in fright as a huge hound dashed in, followed by two men.

It was Pedro, with Captain Pentland and Mackay, the engineer.

Recklessly Pedro bounded over to the corner where Blake lay, his huge tongue licking the detective's hands in an ecstasy of delight.

"Thank Heaven we have found you!" exclaimed the captain, hastening over and shaking Blake's hand.

"Mackay and I, with the dog, have been searching these cursed dens for two days and nights for you! But you are ill! What has happened? Is it serious?"

"Someone took enough interest in me to bury the blade of a knife in my back," smiled Blake, as he dropped the captain's hand and reached for Mackay's.

"Good heavens, you'll meet your death, Mr. Blake, if you go alone into these dens!" replied the captain.

"They nearly got me this time," laughed Blake, rubbing the ears of the hound who had snuggled close against him, his pounding tail and panting sides visible tokens of his joy. "The senorita found me and took care of me," he continued; "and but for her they would have succeeded. But I'll tell you all about it later. In the meantime, can you make arrangements to get me out of here secretly? I don't want it known that they failed in their purpose."

"Yes; I will make arrangements," answered the captain.

"We will get a carriage and transfer you to the hotel tonight. But no one would know you with that growth of beard. And now," went on the captain, shifting nervously, "I'm afraid I've got bad news for you, Mr. Blake. Do you feel strong enough to withstand a shock?"

"Yes—yes.—What is it?" replied Blake. "Tell me, captain."

"Well, it's this way, sir. Captain Brown, of the Orinoco, arrived in port last week. He reported on his arrival that a lad by the name of Gates, travelling alone, had been lost overboard in the North Atlantic two days out. As you told me your assistant was travelling under that name. Thought you ought to know."

"My heavens!" gasped Blake. "Are you sure?"

"Quite, Mr. Blake. I'm sorry to bring you such bad news, but of course, there is always hope that he may have been picked up."

"No—no!" muttered Blake, his eyes filling. "There is little chance of such a thing! Pardon my emotion, gentlemen, but that lad was very dear to me, and I am still a bit weak. But leave me now, and return to-night for me. I wish to be alone."

Slowly they withdrew, the taciturn Mackay furiously blowing his nose. And as the door closed, Blake turned his face to the wall, and, with Pedro's head under his arm, gave himself up to horrible thoughts.

"Poor lad!" he muttered to the dog. "He was such a help and such a companion! What will I do without his sunny ways to cheer me? He had grown so much into my life, and now he leaves it—sent to his death by me!" He groaned involuntarily at the thought. "I've only got you, now, old chap, but together we will avenge him, Pedro! It will go hard with his murderers, for murder it was. Tinker never fell overboard! He was forced over!"

The Spanish woman, who had withdrawn on the captain's entry, returned to the room, and, seeing Blake's dejected attitude, hastened to his side.

"Is the senor feeling worse?" she asked. "Has the visit been too much for him?"

"No, senorita," answered Blake sadly. "My friends brought me sorrowful tidings. One whom I dearly loved is gone from me."

"Was she the senor's wife?" asked the woman.

"No, senorita. I have no wife. It was a young Caballero—a lad."

"I am very sorry, senor!" she replied.

"Thank you! And now, senorita, I must prepare to leave you. My friends come for me this evening."

"Very well, senor. I will lay your things out, and send a lad to help you with your clothes."

The woman left the room, and a few moments later a negro lad entered.

Blake had to rest many times before the last garment was on, but he finally managed it. He tossed the lad a peso, and, sinking into a chair, buried his head in his hands.

The news of Tinker's death had been a great blow to him, and, weak as he was, every move was an effort. Pedro was very dear to him, but Tinker had been a great deal in his life, and he looked forward to the future with an aching heart.

He sat buried in his thoughts until the swift, tropical night had fallen and the woman returned.

She prepared him a strengthening drink, and he had barely finished it when the soft rattle of wheels sounded in the dark, sandy street.

"Well, senorita," said Blake, rising stiffly, "I hardly know how to express my gratitude to you. I wish to reward you for your care for me, and later, when the present blackness of my life has cleared a little, I would do something for you."

"No, senor; I have told you I wish no reward. But listen, senor, before the others come," she went on, speaking rapidly and turning her head. "You, senor, are great and good. The greetings of your friends show me you are honoured among your fellow-men. Senor, I

57

might have been a better woman had I been born in a different atmosphere. You are the first good man I have known. I know that to you I am as nothing; but, senor, there is one reward you can give me, if you will."

"What is it, senorita?" asked Blake gently. "Believe me, if it is possible, I will gladly give it."

"It is this, senor," she whispered, moving closer to him.

"I would have you kiss me once before you go."

Silence reigned for a moment before it was broken by Blake's low voice;

"Senorita, permit me," he said softly, and, bending, gently touched his lips to the woman's forehead.

The wheels stopped as the carriage pulled up at the door, and the captain entered.

"Good-bye, senorita!" Blake said, as he moved away.

"Good-bye, senor! God guard thee! You have been most generous!"

As the door closed, she stumbled to the mattress in the corner and cast herself down in an agony of bitter remorse.

. . . . . .

Blake rapidly gained in strength, and much he needed it, for the days following his departure from the tumble-down house were strenuous ones.

He had a secret interview with Senor Martina, the present head of the Government, and that gentleman had given him the name of the old fisherman who had seen the two boats leave the beach on the night of the president's disappearance.

A conversation with that individual had elicited only one new fact. He was cautious about admitting it, but Blake's tact secured it after an hour's battle of wits. It was that the yacht, in the opinion of the old fisherman, bore a great resemblance to one which had lain in the harbour of Puerto Costa a few weeks previously. He had been chary about admitting the fact, for those aboard the yacht had been intimate with the powers that were, and he did not wish to risk getting himself into trouble.

Blake followed up this point, and had another interview with Senor Martina.

"By the way," remarked Blake, in a casual tone, "I hear there was a yacht in the harbour a short time back. I had some acquaintances cruising in these waters, and have been wondering if it were they."

"Ah! Yes; we had some charming people in port!" replied the old statesman. "A Mr. Grant and his niece. Very wealthy people, I believe. They brought splendid letters with them, and I think we managed to make their stay pleasant."

"Ah! The niece—let me see—I seem to have forgotten her name," murmured Blake.

"Mademoiselle Carston," answered Martina. "A beautiful girl."

"Yes—yes! She is, as you say, a beautiful girl. They still have, then, I presume, the same yacht—The Viking—if I remember rightly?"

"Ah, no. They must have secured a new one, or altered the name, for it was called the Fleur-de-Lys."

"Why, of course! How stupid of me!" laughed Blake. "I remember now. I got the name mixed up with that of another. I am sorry I missed them, but may yet run into them."

And the old statesman, not knowing the double meaning of that last sentence, smiled in answer.

Blake hastened from that interview to the office of the British Consul. There he secured copies of the shipping reports for some weeks back.

It was a long and tedious search, but his eyes lit up with satisfaction as he saw the following item:

"Valparaiso, Chile; Yacht Fleur-de-Lys; Vaughan, master; arrived."

And, dated two days later, was:

"Valparaiso, Chile; Yacht Fleur-de-Lys; Vaughan, master; cleared for Suva, Fiji."

Blake hastened back to his hotel and gave orders to have his bag packed at once.

"Grant—Carston. It may be only a coincidence; but, by heavens, I don't believe it! If Mademoiselle Yvonne isn't at the bottom of this I'll be greatly surprised! And my idea is strengthened since I have discovered that Pearson came from Australia. What on earth is she doing in the South Pacific, and where is she heading for?"

Before he left the hotel, Blake despatched a heavy sealed envelope to Senor Mendoza, in London, and it was addressed to Tinker.

"It's probably useless," he muttered sadly; "but I can't help clinging to the hope that he has been picked up and if he returned to London he would go at once to Senor Mendoza on finding me gone."

Sadly he left the hotel, and quietly joined the Corsair. Captain Pentland had full steam up, and five minutes later the speedy yacht was cutting her way in a southerly direction on what was to be one of the longest chases Sexton Blake had ever had.

THE EIGHTH CHAPTER.   Tinker is Picked Up—He Returns to England—Where is Blake?

THEN Tinker had felt himself dropping through the rain into the dark waters of the Atlantic, he had, as has been said, mechanically clutched his useless weapon.

His senses had been too near the borderland of unconsciousness when his assailant threw him over to distinguish the character of it. But as the air rushed back to his lungs he realised that in his effort he had grasped a lifebuoy. Dodging under it, he came up through the hole, and, resting his arms on the circle, gazed about him as he battled with the waves.

Now far ahead were the lights of the fast-disappearing Orinoco, and even as he gazed she was swallowed up in a heavier deluge of blinding rain.

"This is a pretty situation!" he gasped to himself, as he fought for breath. "What a fool I was to be taken in by a clergyman's outfit, and after the guv'nor warned me so carefully, too! I'll have my work cut out to keep afloat, and it looks like a small chance of being picked up, especially if this rain keeps on. But I don't want to die!" he gasped, as he struggled on. And he was right. He did have his work cut out to keep his head above the waves.

How long he had battled in that tossing, black water he did not know, but a sudden hope grew in his breast as the lights of a ship appeared quite near.

He yelled frantically, but the blinding rain beat down his voice, and as the ship kept on, unheeding, he sank back in despair.

It was perhaps as well for Tinker's nerve that he was unaware that on board that brilliantly-lighted steamer were Blake and Pedro, and that the faithful hound had in some way heard his call for help. Had he known, his despair would have been almost overpowering.

Minutes passed that seemed like hours, hours passed that seemed like an eternity, and still the brave lad battled with the relentless waves.

He lost all count of time, the strain of his constant battle in the cold water was fast numbing his senses.

As dawn broke, he saw what he thought was a sail, and frantically called. His voice came in a hoarse croak, and he sank back with a sob of despair as he saw his reeling senses had enlarged the wings of a gliding seagull to the sail of a ship.

The morning wore on, and Tinker sank into a stupor. Thirst claimed him, and, try as he would, the salt waves found their way into his mouth. Mechanically he battled for breath, but as he sank deeper into a delirium the weary muscles gave up the unequal fight, and he lay back heedless of the green monsters which swept over him.

·　　·　　·　　·　　·

Captain Masters, of the tramp-steamer Annabel, had been at one time one of the smartest captains in the passenger service.

Fate had dogged him, however, with unrelenting steps, and the loss of his ship had reduced him to his present berth.

The wreck was not his fault, and all hands had been saved by his individual efforts, but the loss of a ship is an unpardonable sin in shipping circles, and after a year's total suspension he had been given a seedy tramp-steamer.

But his seamanship had not been impaired, and his keen eyes— perhaps grown keener since the tragedy of his life— searched the sea with their accustomed keen scrutiny.

For that reason, when a small object caught his eye just before dusk shut in, he looked earnestly at it. Reinforcing his naked sight with his telescope, he grunted as the glass confirmed his opinion.

Quickly he sang out an order, and the tramp swung round, heading for the object of his attention.

Again he grunted as they approached it, and lowered a boat.

The sailors returned on deck with the limp figure of a lad, which they laid at his feet.

The captain wasted no time, but went quickly to work. He poured raw spirit between the cold lips, and one of the sailors worked the arms up and down, while another removed the lad's shoes and chafed the cold ankles. Their efforts were rewarded by a faint stirring in the heart region, and as it grew stronger the captain rose.

"Take him up, and put him to bed in the cabin adjoining mine. Give him another dose of spirit, and have the cook prepare hot blankets. He was about gone, but will come round all right now."

He picked up the lifebuoy as they carried the unconscious figure away.

"Orinoco!" he muttered, reading the name painted on it. "She's in the South American trade. Well, I don't know how he got in the water. Perhaps the Orinoco has gone down. In any event, he's going a long distance away from his destination, for I can't land him until I reach Cape Town, and as this magnificent liner isn't equipped with wireless, his friends will have to wait for news."

Tossing aside the lifebuoy, the captain returned to the chart-room, and entered in his log the occurrence which had just taken place.

Tinker, for he was the lad who had been rescued, did not awaken until the following day.

Captain Masters came to see him in the morning, and Tinker gave him a full account of his adventure, concealing only the fact of his real identity.

The kindly man supplied him with extra garments, and before another day had passed Tinker was well enough to come on deck.

His mind was anxious, for he knew Blake would be expecting word from him, but he was very thankful for his escape, and considered himself very fortunate in being rescued at all.

It was nearly three weeks later when they entered Table Bay—that beautiful harbour, guarded by the impressive bulk of the mountain from whence it derives its name.

Tinker thanked the captain earnestly for his goodness, and as he hastened into the town resolved to get Blake, if possible, to use his influence in securing for the captain a better berth, for Tinker had wormed out the story of the captain's life, and his heart had filled with sympathy for the kind-hearted skipper.

Tinker kept the cables warm with his messages.

That night he got only one reply, and it was from Mrs. Bardell, the housekeeper at Baker Street.

"S. B. left same night you left. Heard nothing since. Greatly worried about you both."

Tinker sent an answer to the good soul, and sought the steamship office, his mind full of misgivings about Blake.

He inquired about sailings, and returned to the Grand, where he found another answer. It was from Senor Martina, and read:

"Party mentioned had bad accident. Recovered, and sailed for unknown destination.

"What had I better do?" muttered the lad. "And I wonder what accident the guv'nor had? He must be on the track, though, and he will be nearly crazy about my disappearance. The best thing I can do is to get back to London as quick as I can, and see if he has sent any advice to Senor Mendoza as we arranged."

Rising as he spoke. Tinker hastened back to the steamship-office, where he purchased a ticket.

The next day he was a passenger on the Denley Castle for England.

THE NINTH CHAPTER.   The Re-Union—Blake's Message— Tinker Takes a Journey.

LITTLE less than three weeks later Tinker hastened into the Baker Street apartments.

Mrs. Bardell met him, and her relief at his safe return found vent in a voluble conversation.

Tinker gathered from her stream of talk that nothing had come from Blake, but that there was a cable addressed to Tinker, which she had laid on the desk.

Tinker dashed into the consulting-room, and over to the desk.

It was piled high with the correspondence which had come during Blake's absence, and on the top was the cable.

Tearing it open, he read the terse sentence:

"Go to S. M."

And before the astonished landlady could speak again he had dashed out on a run.

"Well, I calls it strange goings on!" she gasped, as she hastened to the window and saw Tinker hail a taxi.

"They both disappear, and one of 'em comes back looking as though he'd been in the wars, and where the other one is goodness only knows. Now he goes off again, before he's been in the 'ouse five seconds; and when he'll come back again I don't know. They'll both be killed one of these days, I know they will! And what's the use of a woman worrittin' her head about them, when they just won't take care of themselves?"

The kindly soul wiped the corner of her eye as she spoke, and moved about trying to find a spot of dust in the already spotless room.

Tinker took the letters "S. M." to mean Senor Mendoza, and although the cable was unsigned, he knew it must be from Blake.

Senor Mendoza was not at his office in the Embassy, but was in his private apartments.

"Ah, senor," he smiled, as Tinker was announced, "I remember you! I have been expecting you for some days," he said. "And now let me present you to my daughter." Tinker bowed to the beautiful, dark-eyed Spanish girl who sat on a large divan, and the lad could not but sympathise with her as he saw the haunting look of sorrow in her eyes.

Turning to the Minister he stated the reason of his coming, and handed over the cable.

"Yes, I have a letter for you, but must ask you for the code."

Tinker supplied it, and the Minister handed over the letter.

"Leave us, Carmen, please," said Senor Mendoza, to his daughter. "I have some important matters to talk over." The girl rose as he spoke, and, bowing gracefully to both of them, retired.

"If you will excuse me, senor, I will read my letter," said Tinker, as the door closed. "I think it is of importance."

"By all means," replied the Minister, lighting a cigar. Tinker broke the seal, and hurriedly read through the many closely-written sheets, which, he saw, were in Blake's handwriting.

"Well, senor, I hope I am not impertinent in surmising that your letter is from Sexton Blake?"

"Not at all, sir," answered Tinker. "It is from Mr. Blake, and in it he says if I receive it I am at liberty to tell you the contents."

"Ah, thank you!" exclaimed the Minister. "I should be very glad."

The letter was long, the first part being Blake's fears as to Tinker's fate, and, with shining eyes, the lad skipped this portion. Rapidly he gave the Spaniard the gist of what followed, which was a detailed account of Blake's movements, and also the particulars of his chase after the yacht.

"He says here, sir," Tinker added, "that he will put in at Valparaiso for an hour, to see if there is any news to be picked up, and then he will continue the chase to Suva. He says if I get this I had better cable to Suva and travel to Port Said and await instructions. Of course, he fully thinks me dead by now, but he always considers every detail, and it happens I can go to-night without wasting any time."

"I see," remarked the Minister, as Tinker finished. "I agree with you, he is a very thorough man, and has done wonderfully well to pick up the trail so soon. But I wish to show you something. Naturally you understand it is confidential," he added, opening a drawer in his desk and taking out an envelope. "Read that, senor!"

Tinker took the envelope and read the enclosed note. It was the one written by Yvonne to Senorita Mendoza, and Tinker's eyes opened wide as he read it.

"By Jove, sir, it's a cool hand that wrote that! How long since you received it?"

66

"It only came yesterday, and it proves Mr. Blake is on the right track. Now you will remember he forbade my telling my daughter he was working on the case, but in my opinion, things have altered since then, and I want your permission to tell her."

"Well, I don't know—" began Tinker.

"Wait, senor," said the old statesman, raising his hand. "I vouch to you on my honour that she shall not breathe a word, and in addition, I am going to ask you to let us accompany you to Port Said. Then you can cable Mr. Blake we are with you. If he objects, we have nothing to do but return. If not, we will continue on to where you meet him. It is for my daughter's sake I ask, for this strain is nearly killing her."

"Well, in that case, Senor Mendoza, I am sure Mr. Blake would endorse what I do, and I consent with pleasure."

"Thank you, senor," said the Minister, with deep emotion. "I quite realise why you hesitate. And now, when can we start?"

"I will cable Mr. Blake to Suva immediately, and we will catch the Continental train from Charing Cross to-night."

"Good! My daughter and I will be ready. How about joining us here for tea at the Embassy, and we can all leave together?"

"Thank you, sir. I will be delighted," answered Tinker, rising.

Shaking hands with the Minister, he hastened away with a lighter heart to cable Blake.

.   .   .   .   .

That night Tinker, Senor Mendoza, and the beautiful senorita left Charing Cross for the Continent.

At Port Said, Tinker received a long cable from Blake expressing his deep joy at the lad's safety. It was sent from Melbourne, and went on to say they were clearing for Hong Kong. Tinker was to catch the first steamer and hasten on. Blake confirmed Tinker's action regarding Mendoza, and told him by all means to bring them along.

They were fortunate in securing a steamer to Colombo at once, and by the reckless use of money, Senor Mendoza got in touch by cable with the captain of a Hong Kong steamer in the Ceylon port, and arranged to have it held for their arrival.

It was a seedy steamer which they joined there, but Tinker was in high spirits at the early prospect of again seeing Blake, and even the saddened senorita seemed to brighten a bit under the lad's sunny ways.

He spent many hours of that journey telling her of former deeds of Blake's, relegating himself modestly to a very unimportant share.

Consequently it was a fairly cheerful party that steamed into Hong Kong, and Tinker could hardly contain himself when he saw Blake and Pedro on the quay.

It was a memorable meeting between them. Senor Mendoza and the senorita turned away as the lad rushed to the waiting pair, and their eyes wet when they turned back to greet Blake, who was presented to the senorita.

It was a happy re-union on the yacht that night, and none of that cheery party knew of the cloud so quickly to descend again.

Many explanations had to be made. Tinker had to give a detailed account of his adventures, and then Blake took up the conversation.

"The reason I kept my departure for Salvarita from even you, Tinker, was because I knew we had been watched from the moment Senor Mendoza came to see us. I intended to reach Salvarita before you, and meet you there, but as we know events happened to both of us which forbade it."

Blake then recounted his experiences in Puerto Costa up to the time he had started on the chase for the Fleur-de-Lys.

"We headed the Corsair at full speed for Valparaiso," he went on. "I had Captain Pentland stop in there for an hour, but discovered nothing new. I was clinging to the hope that there might be something from Tinker, but I was doomed to disappointment, and needless to say, I took up the chase again with a heavy heart.

"The Fleur-de-Lys had cleared from Valparaiso for Suva, and we sailed at once for that port. Naturally, I had no hopes of overtaking her by then, but I hoped there to pick up the trail.

"Well, you can imagine my surprise on our arrival, when I discovered she had only reached there four days before we had, and had cleared for Melbourne only the day before. Unfortunately we were held up by some necessary repairs to one of the bulkheads, and when we left Suva, the Fleur-de-Lys was four days ahead.

"I had been unable to glean any information in Suva, so of course all we could do was to keep on the trail until we overtook her, and then take steps to find out if our quarry was really on her, or whether we had been on a false trail from the very start.

"On arrival in Melbourne, we discovered she had taken on some electrical material, and had cleared for Hong Kong. The next day we were after her, and when we arrived here found she had left the day previously for Batavia[1]. I discovered here that they endeavoured to secure some electrical supplies, which they were unable to do, and have gone to Batavia for that purpose. For certain reasons, which at present I cannot tell you, I feel more convinced than ever that the people I am after are aboard the Fleur-de-Lys. I know pretty well what their next move will be, and you might be surprised to know that I think we would soon see them if we returned to Suva.

"But on the other hand, I have to guard against unknown details, and for that reason we will sail in" —and he pulled out his watch— "just twenty-two minutes for Batavia. We had to wait an extra day for your arrival, so that gives them two days' start."

"Hadn't you better show the guv'nor that note you showed me, sir?" asked Tinker, turning to Senor Mendoza as Blake finished speaking.

"Ah, yes, certainly! In my interest I had for the moment forgotten it."

He took the note from his pocket, and passed it over to the detective.

"Ah!" exclaimed Blake, when he finished reading it. "I see my deductions are perfectly correct. This endorses them entirely. I now have positive proof that I am right," he said, handing it back.

"Is it asking too much to inquire if you can tell me who is the writer of this?" Senor Mendoza asked.

"I am sorry, but I must disappoint you for the present," replied Blake. "All I can tell you is this. The writer of that note is the cleverest individual with whom I have ever crossed swords. Some day, senor, I may tell you that individual's history, and I promise you it is an interesting story. I have been confident all along that such a gigantic coup could only be carried out by one or two persons, and after reading that note, I have all the proof I desire. And now, senorita and gentlemen, I hear the propeller starting. Let us adjourn to the deck and get our last view of Hong Kong."

---

[1] Jakarta, Indonesia

THE TENTH CHAPTER. Tinker Disappears—Blake Takes a Hand— Blake and Tinker on Board the Fleur-de-Lys.

HONG KONG forms the tip, and beautiful, dirty, cosmopolitan Batavia, the other extremity of that yellow, treacherous, hand-like stretch called the China Sea, of which the Gulf of Siam forms the thumb, and the Java Sea the wrist.

Into the harbour, twisting its way through the many dirty craft and the kaleidoscopic life of the teeming East, steamed the Corsair a few days later.

Blake and Tinker stood on the bridge with Captain Pentland, and the former's eyes lit up with satisfaction as he saw a graceful white yacht standing out from its surroundings, on the bow of which was painted in gilt letters "Fleur-de-Lys."

"The scent grows warm, Tinker," he murmured softly. "And now to ascertain if our quarry is on board, or if we have come on a wild-goose chase, which I think is not likely."

"I say, guv'nor," said Tinker, in an eager tone; "how about my slipping over there after dusk, and trying to discover if they are on board?"

"Well, my lad," smiled Blake; "if you are very careful, I don't mind. But look out they don't handle you as they did before."

"I'll be careful, guv'nor," promised the lad. "I'll be glad of the chance to get back at them for tumbling me into the Atlantic."

"Very well, Tinker; but not a word to the others. For the present I only wish ourselves to know the identity of our quarry."

That evening when the night life of Batavia had begun its course, Tinker slipped quietly over the side, and made his way across the harbour to where the Fleur-de-Lys lay. He was not aware that hardly had he done so, when Blake slipped over after him and followed.

Tinker kept in the shadow and moved cautiously, stepping with great care as he got near the yacht.

Several bales were scattered about the dock, and behind these he took refuge.

Half an. hour passed before anyone stirred on the yacht, and then it was a stout Chinaman who waddled down the gangway and disappeared up the dock.

Tinker judged it to be the yacht's Chinese cook going into the town, where he would probably spend his leave in the opium-clouded atmosphere of some Chinese den; and he was right.

Although the brilliant streams of light came through the saloon portholes, over another hour went by, and still no movement occurred on deck.

Tinker raised himself, and started to make his way cautiously along and endeavour to reach the silent deck, when a soft movement behind caused him to turn.

He gazed into a pair of angry eyes set in a face which was distorted with rage. It was Dr. Rymer, although Tinker did not know it.

Tinker dodged, and started to run, but Rymer shot out his arm, and caught the lad a staggering blow behind the ear.

Tinker had desired to get away without being recognised, but he saw that it was now hopeless. He turned and sprang at his assailant, but through the dark came crashing the heavy butt of a revolver, and he dropped.

Quickly Rymer picked the lad up, and, swinging him over his shoulder, disappeared with his burden up the gangway.

Blake had seen the struggling figures through the gloom, but he had been some distance away when it happened, and when he arrived at the scene of the encounter both participants had gone.

He was positive it must have been Tinker, and was strongly tempted to return to the Corsair and get a party and storm the Fleur-de-Lys. But if by chance he had made a mistake, it would look rather peculiar to go racing aboard a strange yacht with a dozen armed men at his heels.

But he must do something, for if the yacht did contain the people he was after, and if it had been Tinker whom they had captured—well, if they discovered who Tinker was, his plans would all be upset, and Heaven only knew what their next move would be.

Rapidly he thought, and finally a daring plan came to him.

He had seen the fat Chinese cook go ashore. It would be late when he returned, and probably only the watch would be around. They would know where the cook had been, and would pay no attention to him, thinking his mind would be clogged with opium.

Blake would hasten back to the Corsair, and get his own Chinese disguise. This, with the necessary windings to make him as fat as the cook, would serve.

He would watch for the Chinaman's return, and attack him. It would only take a moment to make his face a counterpart of the Chinaman's, and with the latter's clothes he would pass.

Once he had elaborated his plan Blake moved quickly. Softly he hastened back to the Corsair, and got the necessary things.

Captain Pentland had gone into the town, and Senor Mendoza and the senorita had both retired, Ross was in charge, and Blake told him he would be gone for two or three hours as he hurried over the side.

Quickly he made his way back to the Fleur-de-Lys, and, sinking again behind the scattered bales, settled down for a long wait.

All was still and quiet aboard the yacht, and he noticed that during his absence the saloon lights had been extinguished.

The glow of a cigar on the deck told him someone was sitting in its dark shelter.

He dared not light a match and look at his watch, but he calculated an hour must have passed before the glowing cigar-end sailed over the rail into the water, and a scrape and the sound of footsteps indicated the moving away of the invisible smoker.

Another long period passed without movement, and Blake judged it to be near midnight when his quick ears caught the soft shuffle of approaching steps.

"No other man but a Chink walks that way," he breathed to himself as he crept around the bale, and as he gained the other side he crouched low, ready to spring, as through the darkness loomed up the stout, shuffling figure of the Chinese cook.

Blake waited until the Celestial got opposite him, and then, like a panther he threw himself through the air.

He caught the unsuspicious Chinaman in a throttling grip around the throat. The cook squirmed and wriggled under Blake's hold, but the detective was taking no chances of discovery. Pressing his knee in the small of the Chinaman's back, he jerked backwards, and, with a gasping gurgle, the Chinaman yielded and dropped at his feet.

Blake dragged the body to the shelter of a shed some distance away. He hated to treat the man in this way, but Tinker's life was in danger.

Pulling out a small electric torch, he propped it up with its circle of light shining on the unconscious Chinaman's face.

Rapidly Blake worked. A few lines here, a puffing there, a darker shade, a squint to his eyes, the shape of the brows changed, and so perfect had his work been that he could easily have passed in daylight as the unconscious Celestial on the ground.

He quickly appropriated the Chinaman's clothes and slippers, and when he had bound his body to the correct size and had put on his Chinese wig with the Chinaman's hat, he was an exact replica of the senseless cook.

Extinguishing the light, he bent down and hastily bound and gagged his victim, and a moment later he started down the dock towards the Fleur-de-Lys, his feet shuffling along in a perfect imitation of the Chinese walk.

Blake was pleased at the success of his plan so far, but, nevertheless, he kept his revolver in a handy place as he shuffled up the gangway of the yacht.

He had only a vague idea where the cook's quarters were situated, but that was a risk he would have to take.

He was moving along the dark deck in the direction where he thought them to be when a dark figure loomed up and a harsh voice spoke. Blake's heart leaped as he recognised Rymer's tones, but he acted warily, for he knew, with the odds against him, he would have short shrift were his masquerade discovered.

"Here, John!" came Rymer's harsh voice. "This is a nice time to be getting back from leave! We've been waiting for your return to get under way for two hours. I've a good mind to rope-end you! Get below!"

Catching Blake by the shoulders. Rymer hustled him along and sent him sprawling with a kick to the lower deck.

Blake picked himself up, his fingers itching to get at Rymer, but he realised the madness of such a proceeding at the present moment. Bottling up his wrath, he walked to the side and gazed over, his mind working rapidly over Rymer's remark.

"Waiting two hours to get under way!" he muttered. "That means they will soon start, and if I am to do anything I'll have to work quickly. But, my friend, you will suffer for that kick!" he added savagely.

His thoughts broke off, and he looked up as he heard the clang of bells and the sudden churning of the propeller.

"Heavens, they're going now! What a situation! Here am I aboard and Tinker, too! If they discover who we are the game is up. Dare I—can I bluff it out until I get a chance to move? Impossible, but there's nothing else for it. Why didn't I get a dozen men from the Corsair and risk a raid? If they find things out, it will be a quick end for both of us this time."

Swiftly Blake hastened to the other side. There were already several yards of black water between the yacht and the dock, and moving further along, he gazed along the docks, his eyes following the line they would take in leaving the harbour.

"By heavens," he muttered, "we'll pass close to the Corsair! I wonder if I dare risk it?"

A sailor passed at that moment, and threw a curse at the Chinese cook, but Blake paid no attention.

He moved as quick as he dared towards the fo'c's'le, and muttered with relief as he came to the cook's galley.

Two more sailors passed, and Blake snuffled audibly as they went by.

"Oh, you got back, did you, yellow face?" growled one. "A nice temper you have put the skipper in. You'll get that pigtail of yours pulled to-morrow for you!"

"Me velly solly!" answered Blake, in a sing-song voice. "Velly many fliends in Batav."

"You'll wish you didn't have so 'velly many fliends'!" growled the sailor, as he hastened on.

But Blake knew the sailors would not annoy him too much, for, whether it be windjammer or liner, the cook is a personage to treat with respect, particularly at sea, where another cannot be secured. Once more alone, Blake opened the door of the galley and shuffled in, carefully closing it after him. Lighting a match, he searched until he found a candle. This lighted, he darted his eyes around his new quarters.

Though his predecessor had been a Chink, he had been neat, and in that moment Blake blessed him for his neatness, for he could not discern what he hoped to find, and time was more than precious.

That which he was searching for was a piece of paper, and he grunted as his eye caught an old piece of brown wrapping paper in the wood box behind the galley stove.

He set the candle down, and smoothed out the crumpled paper. Pulling out a short piece of pencil, he rapidly wrote:

"Captain Pentland,—Tinker captured. Myself caught on board as yacht sailed. Make for S—. Will endeavour communicate with you there. In greatest haste.—S. B."

"It's a slim chance that we will pass close enough to the Corsair to send this over, but I'll have to take the chance," he muttered.

Feeling in his pocket, he drew out a couple of spare revolver cartridges, and carefully wrapping the note around these, extinguished the candle, and stole outside.

Overhead the stars shone in brilliant tropical splendour. The dainty Fleur-de-Lys was rapidly gaining speed, her sharp bow cutting the water and throwing it out in gleaming phosphorescent foam.

On all sides lay the medley of native craft, over which silence reigned.

Blake crept noiselessly to the bow, and strained his eyes ahead watching for the Corsair.

There she lay far ahead, silent, and unsuspecting of the fate of her two passengers.

Hardened as he was, Blake gasped as the Fleur-de-Lys swung around several points, for he knew if he failed to send his message to the Corsair, he and Tinker had a slim chance of escaping. Even if his message did reach its destination, things would probably reach a crisis long before they could be overtaken.

But it was a chance, even though it was so slim, and that chance he had to take.

Even supposing they did pass close enough for him to throw the note, his greatest fear was that in the darkness it would fall short or go too far.

His taut nerves relaxed again as the yacht swung back, and he saw that the change in her course had been made to avoid a native sampan.

The Corsair was growing more distinct as they swept on, and Blake leaned tensely forward as she drew nearer and nearer.

Would they go close enough? Yes; they would! No; again the Fleur-de-Lys changed her course—no, it was hopeless! Ah, but wait; she was coming round again! Yes; they would pass fairly close! Nearer, nearer—just another cable's-length, As they came opposite, the crouching Blake drew back his hand. Aiming with all his care, he brought his arm forward with all his strength, and released the lead-weighted message.

It sailed through the air, and the detective landed forward, listening tensely for its fall. It came. But was it a flop in the water or on wood? He could not tell, and his heart sank at the torturing thought that it had fallen short.

But he had no more time to investigate, for several sailors tumbled out of the fo'c's'le to take the watch, and the Chinese cook left the rail, and stole noiselessly back to the galley.

THE ELEVENTH CHAPTER.   Sexton Blake, Chinese Cook— Tinker Walks the Plank— Chan to the Rescue.

BLAKE discovered he had tackled one of the biggest propositions in his life, when he went aboard the Fleur-de-Lys disguised as the cook.

He had cause, it is true, to congratulate himself on the perfection of his disguise, for as yet it had created no suspicion, but that was small comfort in the circumstances.

It was the second day out, and as yet he had failed to discover any signs that Tinker was aboard.

One thing, though, he had gained, and that was the proof that his quarry was aboard, and he puzzled his brains over the partnership of Yvonne and Rymer.

Hitherto, they had always worked separately, and Blake had no idea they knew each other.

One had been quite enough to tackle, but with both working together, and on the high seas, with a captain and crew in complete accord with them—well, if his disguise was penetrated, his life shouldn't be worth a minute's purchase.

His only hope was that their suspicions would be killed by the thought that Blake had been put out of the way by their agent, but he knew the slightest thing might bring discovery.

About Graves he did not worry much, for he knew the full extent of any danger to be apprehended from him, Yvonne's uncle ranked far below Yvonne herself in natural shrewdness, and Blake knew it. His methods were less delicate than the woman's, but Blake knew if his disguise were to be penetrated, Graves would be the first to demand his instant death, and would, probably gain his point.

Of the missing president he had seen nothing, and, although he had kept his ears open, the sailors' gossip told him nothing.

He was, for the time, in a very dangerous situation, and absolutely helpless in the camp of the enemy—an enemy who would not hesitate to put an end to him, if necessary.

Little time had he, however, for conjectures, for as has been said, he had tackled a tremendous proposition.

Lucky it was that Blake was an expert cook, for his studies had given him a thorough insight into all methods of cookery. And well he needed it, for he was kept on the jump.

Up at five every morning to prepare the sailors' breakfast. Then at night, the saloon breakfast had to be prepared.

At eleven, beef-tea for the upper deck. Twelve brought the sailors' dinner-time, and one the saloon lunch.

Hardly had he cleared up from this, when afternoon tea had to be served on deck, and the stewards kept him busy. The sailors' supper came at five-thirty, and the saloon dinner at seven, after which a cold supper had to be served at nine.

Truly he had tackled a proposition if you will, and although he was prepared to do anything to run down a quarry rather than write the word failure in his book, he was heartily sick of the situation at the end of the second day.

He smiled grimly, as he thought of the situation, for, dangerous as was his position, he had to confess that it contained an element of humour, and his smile still broadened when many rough compliments were thrown at him from the fo'c's'le on the improvements of his cooking.

To complicate matters, his first morning had brought to light an unexpected inheritance from his predecessor in the shape of a young Chinese "cookee," whose English vocabulary extended to the one word "allight," which he monotonously emitted, when the sailors addressed him. Luckily, Blake knew Chinese, and he spent half an hour with the astonished boy in strenuous diplomacy, for the young Celestial had discovered at once the difference in accent. But when he had finished, Blake had secured a firm adherent who eventually proved a useful ally.

Blake had not seen any signs of Tinker for a very good reason, but the evening of the second day was to bring him those signs, and their coming was to send the detective through a sharper and swifter agony of mind than he had ever experienced.

When Tinker had been carried aboard by Rymer, he had been conveyed to a cabin, and unceremoniously tossed into a bunk. For two days the stress of affairs had prevented the investigation of his conduct, as it was thought he had been only a curious loafer. Rymer had carried him aboard merely to be on the safe side, and little did he dream that he had captured the lad whom he thought at the bottom of the Atlantic. He would not have recognised Tinker if he had seen him; but Yvonne, Graves, and Captain Vaughan knew him well, not counting Hendricks, the mate.

Consequently, he had been left undisturbed, except for the visits of the steward who brought his meals.

Tinker was aware they were at sea, but his porthole only showed a weary stretch of waves, and for that reason he welcomed the gruff command to come to the saloon. It would at least be a break in the monotony; but, brave as the lad was, he would have clung to that monotony as a haven of delight had he known the fate in store for him.

The saloon was brilliantly lighted. Yvonne sat lounging in her favourite chair—Graves was smoking in another, while Rymer loafed restlessly about.

Tinker's conductor left him at the door, and the lad blinked his eyes as he stumbled in.

Yvonne and Graves threw off their languid attitude, and sat up with a jerk as Tinker walked over and stood in front of them. Rymer, seeing something unusual was in the wind, stopped prowling about, and walked closer.

"So," said Yvonne, "we meet again, my young friend. I thought you were safely at the bottom of the sea by now."

"It is no fault of mademoiselle's that I am not," retorted Tinker, as evenly as Yvonne had spoken.

"Your spirit has evidently not suffered," she went on.

"Are you of the feline tribe, that you have so many lives?"

"As to that, mademoiselle, I will leave you to guess. As for my spirit, you may bend it, but you and all your associates cannot break it!"

"Truly, my lad, your late master had reason to be proud of you," returned Yvonne, her eyes softening. "Come, I will give you freedom, give you wealth, and give you life, if you will join us. What do you say?"

"Look here, Yvonne," said Graves, "you're too chicken-hearted. We evidently failed the first time, and this time he must go!"

"Don't interfere, please!" replied Yvonne coldly. "I trust I am still at the head of affairs. As yet I have not been responsible for the taking of a life, unless it be Bechstein's suicide, a fate which he deserved. You issued the instructions to have Sexton Blake and this lad removed, and when it was too late to alter matters I countenanced it.

"But I do not believe in assassination. If I had met Sexton Blake in fair fight, and his removal had been essential, I would have taken the necessary step—but to knife a man in the back, no; nor will I permit any member of the circle to do it. Now, my lad," she added, turning to Tinker, "what do you say, will you join us?"

"Mademoiselle," answered Tinker, "it is impossible! Believe me, Sexton Blake had a high respect for you, and I am glad to hear that you were not responsible for the attacks on us. I am young, mademoiselle, and don't wish to be impertinent, but instead of my joining you, I would suggest you come over to the side of the law. I have heard Sexton Blake say you would have made a great detective."

"You speak boldly, my lad," answered Yvonne, "but you conjure with a powerful name. You are too young to understand how, but enough—if you won't join us, you will have to remain a prisoner! Now leave me, and I will consider your case."

She rang as she spoke, and sent Tinker away with the man who answered.

Rising, she bowed coldly to her uncle and Rymer, and swept away to her own cabin.

She did not see the blazing look of jealousy in Rymer's eyes when she told Tinker that he had conjured with a powerful name when he used that of Sexton Blake. Nor did she know that those words had created in Rymer a deadly enmity against Tinker.

For Rymer had fallen hopelessly in love with Yvonne, and her coldness towards his advances had only added fuel to the flame. Some instinct had told him that Sexton Blake had received her love, and the remark she had made had brought his jealousy to fever heat.

He had concealed the tempest of his emotions as Yvonne rose and departed, but as the door closed he turned with a snarl to Graves.

"It seems," he said, "that you are right. Mademoiselle is getting chicken-hearted!"

"Yes; and it's a big mistake!" growled her uncle. "If I had my way, I'd get rid of him while we have him in our clutches. Experience ought to have taught her the danger of not doing so. But she will ruin herself and the whole lot of us with her quixotic notions of honour."

"I agree with you," replied Rymer. "Why shouldn't we take the law into our own hands? I am vice-president, and you are secretary and treasurer. Surely our own mutual decision for the good of the circle ought to go?"

He leaned forward and gazed craftily at Yvonne's weak uncle, and the latter, always yielding to Rymer's dominating will, gave in.

"Gad! There'll be the deuce of a row when she finds out!" he muttered.

"She'll come round all right," replied Rymer confidentially, seeing he had won. "I tell you I won't rest until every sign of Sexton Blake is swept from my path!" he added savagely.

"How will we do it?" inquired Graves.

"I've thought it all out," answered Rymer. "Listen! Mademoiselle has gone to retire. We will give her half an hour, and then we will take our young friend on deck. And this time, believe me, there will be no mistake. We will put out a plank, as the pirates of old used to do, blindfold him, and bind his hands, and he will walk that plank! I guess that'll send him under to stay this time."

Graves nodded, and the two silently left the saloon.

Yvonne, it is true, was against the laws of society, but her outlawry was confined to what she considered the meting out of just punishment to those who had ruined her mother and herself. She had accepted all the conditions of such a life, and when necessary, would in fair fight, countenance a killing.

Perverted and wrong her ideas certainly were, but it had been the fault of those whose punishment she was now endeavouring to bring about. But she had a strict code of honour and scrupulously lived up to it. It was that which claimed such a deep admiration from Sexton Blake, and it had been an additional shock to Yvonne's proud nature when Blake had refused her hand.

His heart would have softened towards the wayward girl had he known the intense suffering she had experienced since she believed him dead. But we sum Yvonne up best, perhaps, when we say she ran straight, and with the exception of her wrong ideas of taking the law into her own hands, her honourable and upright nature would have been a credit to many on the side of the law and order.

But the two men who had just quitted the saloon were not troubled by any such ideas; but in acting as they did, in direct defiance to Yvonne's orders, and the underhand methods they used, they broke the salient law which holds criminals, as well as other orders, together—honour with each other, and the breaking of which invariably spells ruin.

Tinker had breathed easier at Yvonne's words, and his heart had filled with a great sympathy toward her. Consequently, he got a rude shock when the door of his cabin opened, and he was roughly seized and his arms bound behind him. His captors, two husky seamen, dragged him on deck, and led him along to the after port.

He gasped with sudden dread as he saw the plank sticking out over the dark waters, and read their fiendish purpose.

To do him justice, he never for a moment suspected Yvonne had gone back on her word, and had issued orders for his death. He knew that in some way her lieutenants had taken the law into their own hands. If he could attract her attention, he might yet be saved. Opening his mouth he started to yell, but a heavy hand descended, choking it off in a low gurgle.

Swiftly they bound a handkerchief around his mouth, and another over his eyes..

Tinker gritted his teeth, and brought all his manhood to bear and keep his nerve and die bravely. But he had had one awful experience in the ocean, and dreaded another. Then, he had had a fighting chance, but now he must die like a dog. His thoughts raced back to Blake and Pedro, and he struggled valiantly to suppress a choking sob, for life had been very dear to him since he had lived with Blake, and he was young.

But no relief came to him, and with a fervent prayer for courage to hang out he set his foot on the plank.

Slowly, and with an awful agony of suspense, he shuffled along the plank, but before he had covered half its length the men at the side of the yacht tipped it up, and the helpless lad dropped into the shark-infested waters.

Blake was sitting in the darkness of his galley when the unusual stir told him something out of the ordinary was happening.

He had cautiously slipped along the deck, crouching low as he saw in the glare of a lantern the circle of men at the rail.

He gasped in horror when he saw Tinker led up and bound. The plank told its own story, and the beads came out on the detective's forehead as he saw the lad's impending fate.

He worked his way back to the bow, and searched feverishly until he found a long coil of rope.

Shouldering it, he whispered softly to the Chinese boy, to whom he spoke rapidly in guttural Chinese.

The boy nodded as eagerly as his nature would permit, and the celestially-attired pair crept back along the deck, Blake carrying the long coil of rope.

He had counted on the interest of the men at the rail in their occupation to assist his purpose, and he calculated rightly, for, absorbed in their fiendish work, they did not see the gliding Orientals who crept by on the opposite side and made for the stern.

Rapidly Blake uncoiled the rope, and secured one end firmly to the rail, the other end he tied around the boy's waist.

"You are sure, Chan, that you are a sufficiently strong swimmer?"

"Oh, yes, master! Many years have I dived in the waters for pearls."

"Very well, my lad. I would go myself, but you would not be strong enough to pull me back. Chan, don't miss him!" he added, the sweat breaking out again on his forehead. "If you succeed, your reward will be great; and if you fail—well, I swear I will destroy every being on this yacht."

Solemnly he whispered the words, and a moment later Chan went over the side ready to slip into the water.

Blake crept up, and stared back tensely, and gasped as he saw the helpless, blindfolded Tinker start on his awful journey.

Hastening back, he stood at the rail, and never had Sexton Blake passed through the eternity of agony through which he went that moment.

It seemed a year before the splash came, and he had no need to give the signal to the Chinese boy; for he also had heard it, and his slim body cut the water like an arrow as he dived silently.

Blake grasped the rope, gritting his teeth to control himself. He heaved back as he felt a tug, and gazed with intensity at the black water. But no head showed above it, and his heart contracted with fear as he looked for the sign of success or failure.

Chan had dived in order to try and grasp Tinker as he went past. But it would be very easy to fail in that black water, and, as the yacht was travelling at high speed, if he failed once, the helpless lad would soon be far astern in those shark-infested waters.

Blake's jaws worked as he saw Chan's head come up, and he momentarily raised his eyes in a great wave of thankfulness as the boy's laboured struggles told him he had a burden.

Desperately he pulled in on the rope until the boy was underneath.

A great length of the slack rope now looped along behind, and the resourceful Chinese boy soon had it looped around his burden.

Blake pulled again, his arms straining with the dead weight. But he had the strength of two men that night, and the strong man gave a dry sob of relief as he drew the inanimate Tinker over the rail.

He tied the rope to the rail, and Chan rapidly squirmed up it hand over hand.

Silently they bent over Tinker. His would-be murderers had not known when they tied the handkerchief over Tinker's mouth that it would eventually be a help to the lad, but such it was, for it had helped to keep the water from entering his lungs. Blake worked rapidly, and breathed easier when Tinker's lids fluttered, and finally opened.

He stared in amazement at the Chinaman bending over him, but his eyes filled with joyous tears as Blake whispered a few words.

It was a long and dangerous trip from the stern to the cook's galley in the bow, but the little band managed it.

Blake gave Tinker a dry outfit, and concealed him in the privacy of his own galley, where, unless something out of the ordinary occurred, he would be moderately safe.

He gripped Chan's hand in deep gratitude as the Chinese boy departed, and then sat down to bring his keen mind into full play in an endeavour to solve the problem.

And well was it for Sexton Blake that he had the asset of such a mind in such a position.

THE TWELFTH CHAPTER.   The Mystery of the Water Tanks—Blake Makes a Purchase—Blake Captures the Fleur-de-Lys.

SEVERAL days passed safely, and the detective began to breathe easier.

Blake expected every day that the concealed Tinker would be discovered, but his predecessor had evidently impressed the sailors with the fact that he would not have them in his galley, for, with the exception of their trips at meal-time to have their plates filled, they gave the galley a wide berth.

What was their destination he had no idea, but he was able to form a rough notion of their position from the talk of the sailors.

In this way he had known when they passed through the Torres Straits, and likewise a few evenings later he heard one of the sailors remark that New Caledonia lay off the starboard side.

That night Blake spent several hours in deep thought.

He had discovered for a positive fact that President Pearson was not aboard, and the problem was where and when had he been set off?

He went over the steps of the chase point by point. He could place every movement of the Fleur-de-Lys with the exception of one period.

Her journey from Valparaiso to Suva had consumed an extraordinarily long time, for, although she had over two weeks' start from Salvarita, Blake had reached Suva only four days after her arrival. That pointed to a blank time to be filled up by some movement of the yacht. He figured it was almost certain that she had stopped somewhere between Valparaiso and Fiji, but the point was where?

That stoppage would give the necessary opportunity for disposing of the president and the bullion. What strengthened the detective's theory that she had stopped somewhere was the fact that she had continued on to Melbourne, Hong Kong, and Batavia, and in each place had taken in heavy supplies. Then, instead of proceeding to Europe, she had started back toward the South Pacific, and now Fiji lay just ahead.

Certainly it pointed to some destination in the South Pacific. The detective had no idea as to whether Captain Pentland had received his hastily-written note. If he had not Blake was in a hard situation. He must get word to the captain in some way, but the problem was how?

Long and persistently he turned the problem over and over in his mind, and finally adopted a plan which, though risky, seemed the only one with a chance of success.

Late that night, when all hands but the watch were wrapped in slumber, the stout Chinese cook would have surprised his shipmates by his athletic actions. He seemed to be performing stealthy feats of agility in the neighbourhood of the water tanks, and the result of his midnight journey was demonstrated at breakfast-time the next morning.

The first sign came from the sailors. One and all they spat out their coffee in disgust, and an indignant deputation waited on the cook.

"There," growled the spokesman of the party, poking his cup under Blake's nose. "Wot do yer call that mess, yall'er-face?"

"Cloffee—vely good cloffee!" replied Blake, with an expansive Celestial smile.

"Oh, it is 'velly good,' is it? Well, just you taste it, old yaller-face, and see how 'velly good' it is!"

The sailor thrust the cup at Blake, who tasted it, and hurriedly spat it out.

"Velly bad—velly bad!" he answered, in a sing-song toney "Sailor quite light! Me no undelstand."

"Well, you'd better jolly quick understand!" growled the sailor, partially mollified by the cook's acknowledgment as to its badness.

"Me no undelstand!" sang Blake. "Me make it same as all time. Come, I show you!"

The sailor entered the galley, and watched Blake rapidly mix fresh coffee. He poured it out as he finished, and handed the cupful to the sailor. That worthy put it to his lips, but a comical look of disgust came over his face as he set it back hurriedly and hastened outside.

"You see," said Blake, "it is not my fault."

"Well, give me a cup of water until I wash this taste out," growled the sailor, "and then we'll see Captain Vaughan."

Blake did as he was bid, but, as the sailor took a deep draught, getting the full benefit of the awful acid taste, it was the last straw.

Dashing the cup to pieces on the deck, he fairly danced with rage.

"It's the water, you bloomin' old yaller fiend. Wot in blazes 'ave yer put in it?"

"Me put nothing," protested Blake innocently.

"Well, it's rotten!" gasped the sailor, "Come on, boys, and investigate it."

The sailors hurried to the water tanks, and drew off a pailful from each. But their efforts were barren of success, for every tank was tainted with the peculiar acid taste.

The party of seamen hastened to the captain and informed him of the state of affairs.

Captain Vaughan himself descended and investigated the tanks, but his results were the same as those of the seamen.

He hastened away to inform Yvonne, and, returning a few moments later, informed the seamen that they would head at once for Suva to have the tanks overhauled and take in fresh water, and that in the meantime they would all have to get along on distilled water for the time being.

"It is a mystery how the water has become tainted," he wound up. "Someone may be playing a practical joke on us, but if I find out who it is I'll show him the joke of a rope's-end. Now, get on with your work, boys, and as quickly as I can get some water distilled I will have the cook prepare you a breakfast. In the meantime, you will all be served out an extra round of rum."

The sailors cheered, and returned to their work; and in the cook's galley the stout Chinese cook smiled, for he had gained his point, and they would stop at Suva.

The yacht made Suva the next day, and the cook found it necessary to obtain leave to go ashore for a few things for the galley.

He explained matters to the concealed Tinker, and, leaving Chan on guard, hastened over the side.

Blake made his way to the British Consul, and binding that astounded gentleman to secrecy, left a letter with him to be delivered to Captain Pentland on his arrival, for a perusal of the shipping news disclosed the fact that the yacht Corsair had cleared from Batavia bound for Suva, Fiji, and he knew his first note had miraculously landed on the deck.

In the note he explained his suspicions to Captain Pentland, and told him to remain at Suva, where the detective would endeavour to communicate with him later.

It would have simplified matters wonderfully if Blake could have had Yvonne and her companions arrested at Suva; but, unfortunately, he had no positive proof as yet that they had abducted President Pearson, and, besides, Salvarita had no extradition law with Great Britain.

Consequently, all he could do was to stick to the trail until he discovered the missing president, and in the mean time, give every attention to details.

On leaving the British Consul's Blake made his way to a chemist's, and there purchased a box of harmless-looking white powder. Then, making a few purchases as his excuse for being ashore, he hastened back to the yacht, his box of white powder concealed in the flowing sleeve of his capacious jacket.

Tinker was still undiscovered when Blake returned, and that evening, with her tanks cleaned and replenished, the Fleur-de-Lys once more got under way.

Three days later a dark cloud appeared on the eastern horizon, and as the day wore on the sailors clustered eagerly in the bow.

Blake left the galley and moved to the rail, his eyes as inscrutable as a genuine Chinaman's, but his ears open for any remarks.

"I'll be jolly glad to get back to the island!" remarked a sailor near him.

"So will I!" answered another. "It means a rest and good food and a jolly good time."

"We ought to make the lagoon about eight," returned the first.

"Not much," replied his companion. "I heard the captain say we'd drop anchor at ten."

Blake turned casually, and returned to his galley. At least he had definite information, and a move must be made soon.

As the afternoon wore on he started preparing the evening meal, and, strange to say, in all the food, both for the saloon and the fo'c's'le, he put a large portion of the white powder he had purchased in Suva.

He did not wish to have it affect the sailors before dinner had been served in the saloon, as suspicion would be aroused and his plans upset.

Consequently, the sailors' supper was not ready until six that night. But the seamen were in a good humour at the prospect of early release, and only a few mild curses greeted the cook's unpunctuality.

Seven arrived, and dinner was sent into the saloon promptly on time. Half-past seven came, and for men who had not had a hard day, the sailors seemed to be suddenly seized with an extreme weariness, for first one and then another started yawning prodigiously.

Those who were not on watch gave in to the demand of their heavy lids, and sought the fo'c's'le, where they threw themselves out on their bunks.

Almost before they had settled themselves they were in a heavy sleep.

Those on watch battled valiantly to overcome their sudden sleepiness, but first one and then another succumbed and dropped helplessly to the deck.

Blake smiled as he saw the effects of his powder, but he looked for quicker results in the saloon, for he had made their dose particularly stiff, and had given less to the sailors, in order that they should not succumb before the saloon dinner had been served.

He had not long to wait, for a few minutes later a scared-looking steward dashed out from the saloon, and headed for the cook's galley.

"What in blazes have you done?" he gasped as he reached Blake. "Everyone has gone to sleep at the table."

His answer was a sudden spring from Blake, and to render him helpless was the work of only a moment.

Blake dragged him into the galley, and there hastened to release Tinker.

"Now, my boy, we've got our work cut out for us," he said, as he passed Tinker a revolver. "There are five more stewards to settle yet, for they haven't had their supper, and will be unaffected. Then we've got Hendricks, the mate, who is on the bridge, and the mate at the wheel. The engineer and his assistants can wait, for they won't be up yet for another half-hour. Are you ready?"

"Yes, guv'nor, you bet I am! Crikey, but you have scored!" he said, with a look of admiration at the detective.

"But just let me get at them! I've got several scores to settle with them!"

Blake smiled grimly, as he led the way to the saloon.

Yvonne sat with her head resting in her hand, fast asleep. All around sat Captain Vaughan, Rymer, and Graves in a similar condition.

But Blake and Tinker lost no time. Two stewards were endeavouring to awaken the sleepers, and their hands went up quickly as Blake levelled his revolver.

Tinker quickly bound them, and they proceeded to find the others.

Two were getting the cabins ready for the night, and these received the same treatment as their fellows. As they went along the passage the last steward appeared with his arms full of linen, and he also was bound.

"Now for the bridge. Tinker!" jerked Blake.

They hastened up the companion way, and along the deck to the bridge companion.

They crept up softly, but Hendricks and the man at the wheel were as yet unsuspicious.

The mate was pacing up and down, and his eyes opened in amazement as he saw the supposed Chinese cook with a levelled revolver in his hand.

"Here, you yellow-skinned dog! What do you mean?" he snapped angrily. "Get below at once!"

"Not just yet, Mr. Hendricks!" answered Blake coolly.

Hendricks' eyes dilated as he heard Blake's voice, but that was mild compared to the look of horror on his face as he saw Tinker appear.

Up went his hands, for he saw they meant business; and Tinker's uncanny appearance, when by all calculations he ought to have been at the bottom of the ocean, took his breath away.

"Now walk to the wheelhouse, Hendricks!" snapped Blake.

Hendricks did so, his hands still aloft.

"Now, Tinker," continued Blake, "go below and get Chan! Then get some rope, and tie up every one on the yacht, with the exception of mademoiselle! Carry her to her cabin, and lay her in her bunk. Then lock her in. After you have done that, go on guard at the entrance to the engine-room, and the first man who appears secure him! Don't run any risks. If he fights, disable him. You will know how," he added grimly. "I will attend to this pair myself."

"Right, guv'nor!" responded Tinker. "I promise you I'll settle them this time!"

"Now, Mr. Hendricks," snapped Blake, pulling out a cigar and lighting it with one hand, "you will keep on in exactly the same course! You will instruct the man how to enter the lagoon, and if you don't do just exactly that in every detail, I promise you I will deal with you in a way you won't like! And you know whether I mean what I say or not."

"Oh, I know when I'm beaten!" growled Hendricks surlily. "I'll take you into the lagoon all right. But I'd like jolly well to know how you've overpowered the whole crew."

"I don't mind in the least telling you," answered Blake coolly. "They had a sudden desire for sleep, which, strange to say, invaded the saloon as well. They succumbed to it, that is all. And now, Hendricks, no more talk, please!"

The man at the wheel had gazed in open-mouthed astonishment at the "hold up," but on Blake's ordering him to keep the yacht's head as she was, he swallowed his fear and curiosity and attended to the wheel.

Blake leaned against the rail, his revolver ready for business.

Two hours later Tinker came up to report that all hands had been secured, and that one of the engineer's assistants had also been secured on making his appearance on deck.

As the lad finished his report the yacht swung into the opening of the lagoon.

Hendricks, at Blake's orders, signalled the engine-room to stop and she floated ahead by her own impetus. Blake, leaving Tinker to keep the wheelman covered, forced Hendricks at the point of the gun to the lower-deck, and compelled him to release the anchor.

Calling Chan, he ordered the Chinese boy to bind the mate, and that grinning individual seemed delighted at the job, for he had received many kicks from Hendricks in days past.

Blake ascended again to the bridge, in order to secure the wheelman, after which the triumphant trio made their way to the engine-room.

The astonished engineer and his remaining assistant, however, were not to be taken without a fight, and picked up heavy wrenches as weapons.

But Blake was in no mood to lose any time, and his revolver spoke sharply, disabling the engineer's arm. The assistant, seeing the fate of his chief, gave in, and a moment later the last of the yacht's company lay helpless on the engine-room floor.

Blake, Tinker, and Chan returned to the deck, and Blake heaved a sigh of satisfaction as he surveyed the scene of his success.

THE THIRTEENTH CHAPTER. Yvonne Completes Her Revenge — Blake Finishes the Chase—Unmasked—The End.

BUT Blake and Tinker were by no means out of the wood yet.

Through the trees fringing the shore of the lagoon came the gleam of lights.

"That's their hiding-place," remarked Blake, "and the question is, Tinker, how many have been left in charge?"

"It doesn't seem as though they would leave many, guv'nor," answered Tinker.

"No, it doesn't, my lad; but, on the other hand, we don't know. It is true, the island may be uninhabited; but in that house yonder they have probably got the missing president, and there must be, at least, half a dozen in charge. It is strange no one has appeared to meet the yacht, but as we came in without lights, and did not whistle, they may not have noticed us yet. However, we've got to investigate, so let's get along."

Rapidly they worked the davits, and a moment later the small boat hit the water. The three skimmed down the ropes, and cast off.

Chan was an expert at the oars, and he pulled noiselessly over the dark stretch between the yacht and the shore.

They grounded silently, and Blake led the way through the trees in the direction of the lighted house.

As they approached, they saw moving figures in what they judged to be the dining-room, and Blake crept forward to investigate.

He gave a start of satisfaction as he saw a man with iron-grey hair at the table whom he knew to be President Pearson.

A man was serving him, and another man with a rifle stood near the door.

Blake crept back to his companions, and told them what he had seen.

"My idea is to make a rush for the front door, and take them by surprise. They will think it is only their returned companions, and we stand a chance of succeeding."

Leading the way, Blake walked up on the wide balcony, and opened the front door.

Tinker and Chan came close behind, and they got clear to the open door of the dining-room without being challenged,

"Hands up—quick!" snapped Blake, as he entered.

And the rifle of the astonished guard fell with a clatter to the floor as his hands went up. The serving-man dropped the plates he was carrying, and followed suit, while the president gazed in amazement at the stout Chinaman with the levelled revolver.

"It's all right, President Pearson," smiled Blake. "Permit me to introduce myself. I am Sexton Blake, and must confess I have had a long chase to find you. But later for that. Can you tell me how many more there are?"

"Yes, Mr. Blake," replied the relieved president. "There are two more, I think. But allow me to thank you for your success in finding my whereabouts."

Blake smiled, and, picking up the fallen rifle, handed it to the president.

"I don't suppose you will object to keeping guard over these two while we find the others," he remarked.

"That I won't!" answered the president. "And if they move a hand, Heaven help them!" he added, grimly.

They found the remaining two in the lower regions of the house, and, securing them, dragged them to the dining-room.

The guard and the serving-man were then bound, and Blake and Tinker, who were weary and hungry from the strenuous evening, joined the president at the table.

Chan investigated the kitchen, and served a very passable meal to the victors, and while they ate Blake heard the president's story, but what he did not hear from that gentleman was the reason of his abduction.

After dinner they worked late into the night transferring to the yacht the prisoners and the bullion, which they found still intact in a large vault.

Blake sent the president into the engine-room with Tinker to help him. The detective himself, who had carefully studied the yacht's chart of the lagoon entrance, took the wheel. Chan reigned supreme in the cook's galley. As dawn broke in golden splendour over the palm-fringed lagoon Blake rang the starting bell, and the Fleur-de-Lys, clipping her dainty nose into the pearly waters, headed out of the lagoon, manned by her small but victorious crew.

Blake headed the yacht for Fiji, and at the end of the first day he entered the wireless-room to endeavour to get in touch with the Corsair. He was not able to do so until the following morning, but shortly after daybreak he got a clear answer.

Rapidly he sent the message, informing Captain Pentland of his position, and instructing him to put to sea and meet them in mid-ocean.

An affirmative reply came back, and early the following evening the two yachts met.

Captain Pentland sent the Corsair's second officer and a prize crew aboard to take charge of the Fleur-de-Lys and her prisoners, but before turning them over officially to President Pearson to be taken to Salvarita for punishment, Blake had two interviews.

Yvonne had been released at once on her recovery from the effects of the sleeping-draught which Blake had administered. She had passed her word not to attempt to hinder his plans nor to release her companions, and once again Blake had accepted that strange girl's word.

She had been dumbfounded at seeing Blake alive, and, regardless of the peril in which she stood and the apparent failure of her plans, she was filled with a reckless gaiety caused by her deep relief that he still lived.

Blake had invited her to a place opposite him at the table, and as the president did not have his meals at the same hour, Yvonne was free from the restraint of his presence.

The consequence was that in her reckless mood all her innate charm came to the surface.

It was hard to realise that their positions were those of captor and prisoner, and when her shapely bronze head disappeared through the door Blake marvelled at the deserted air of everything, and the odd sense of loneliness which came over him.

Just before they met the Corsair, Blake called Yvonne into the saloon and spoke to her.

"Mademoiselle," he said, "I find that although you planned the abduction of the president and the removal of the bullion, that you were not responsible for the attempt on my life and that of my assistant, and, on the contrary, you forbade the use of violence the second time Tinker fell into your hands. For that reason, mademoiselle, I wish to say that I can offer you freedom, but not that of your companions."

Yvonne drew herself up as she replied.

"Thank you, Mr. Blake," she said quietly. "'But I do not desire my freedom. I have stood by my companions and will do so to the end. It would be cowardly and dishonourable for me to accept your offer and to leave them to suffer the punishment. I thought you knew me better than that."

"I took it for granted, mademoiselle," answered Blake "that such would be your answer. I admire your sense of honour at the same time regretting it should have to be brought into play under such circumstances."

"I know you will never see my point of view," she replied. "But as for the second attempt on the life of your assistant, I do not plan murders. Had I known in time it never would have happened. How you saved him I don't know; but both Rymer and my uncle would have suffered for that act on my arrival at the island. Rymer I would have put in irons, and landed in Europe or South America at the first opportunity; but, as things have turned out, I will stick by them. We are not in the Salvarita prison yet," she added saucily, "and I promise you I will endeavour to release my companions as soon as you turn us over to the president. If I succeed I will drop Rymer at once, for I don't desire a member of his calibre. Besides," she added, dropping her eyes, "his attentions were getting altogether too persistent."

And Sexton Blake, man of ice, for some unaccountable reason, felt a sudden desire to drop violent hands on the absent Rymer.

"I am glad you offered me my freedom before you turned me over to Pearson," went on Yvonne. "For the present I cannot explain, but I will do so before you leave. You said, I think, that Senor Mendoza and his daughter were aboard the Corsair?"

Blake nodded.

"Very well; I wish to ask as a favour that you will bring the senorita over to the Fleur-de-Lys and arrange a few minutes' conversation for me. I would like you to be present, and, above all, President Pearson."

"I think I can grant your request, mademoiselle," smiled Blake. "You have been a very good prisoner, and deserve a reward."

Thus it came about that after the prize crew had taken charge of the yacht, Yvonne, the senorita, Blake, and Pearson met in the saloon.

Yvonne leaned against the table facing them, and wasted no time in beginning.

"You all wonder, perhaps," she began, "why I have requested you to grant me these few moments—all, perhaps, except you, James

Pearson."

Pearson opened his mouth to speak, but Blake silenced him with a gesture.

"My reason is threefold," continued Yvonne. "One is my desire that you, Mr. Blake, shall understand why I abducted the president; the second, that Senorita Mendoza shall understand exactly the kind of man he is; and thirdly, that you, James Pearson, will suffer still more for your sins."

"I protest!" cried Pearson. "Senorita, I beg of you to refuse to listen to the tales of this adventuress!"

Again Blake silenced him, and Yvonne, looking at Pearson with contempt, went on:

"Adventuress; yes, perhaps! But who made me one? Listen, senorita, and I will tell you who the noble President Pearson is!"

Rapidly Yvonne told the story of how Pearson, with Vineburg, and the other directors of the Jig Saw Mine in Australia, had ruined her mother and herself by their swindles, causing her mother's death from shock. Of how the law would not reach them, and how she had been driven into the world penniless and her heart full of bitter desire for revenge; of how she had made money, backing horses, and how she had started on her campaign of retribution; how she had picked Vineburg as the first to be revenged upon, and how he having changed his name to Bechstein, had committed suicide. Then how Pearson was the next on the list, and the result of the attempt on him.

"Now, senorita," finished Yvonne, "if you still desire to marry him, I wish you joy of your bargain. You may think me cruel to tell you this, but it is for your own good."

Blake had heard the tale from Yvonne when he had captured her in the Bechstein case, and he had had a shrewd suspicion that Pearson may have been mixed up in the deal.

He turned and looked with contempt at the big, loose-jointed man, who stood with beads of perspiration on his forehead.

"Don't believe her, senorita!" he snarled. "I swear to you they are all lies!"

The senorita had not spoken as she listened to Yvonne's indictment of Pearson, and only the laboured heaving of her breast told of her intense emotion.

As Pearson spoke she looked at him, and then turned to Blake.

"What do you say, Senor Blake—are they lies?"

"I have never had any occasion to doubt mademoiselle's word," answered Blake quietly, "and I see no reason to doubt her word now."

The senorita turned to Pearson, her dark eyes flashing with anger.

"It seems, senor," she said, in a tense voice, "that I gave my trust and love to a contemptible cad! My one hope is that I may be able to wipe every recollection of you from my mind, for what was once love has now turned to loathing! A swindler of women, and you dare to offer marriage to a Mendoza! Mademoiselle, I thank you! Permit me to retire!"

Bowing, the disillusioned and angry senorita swept from the saloon, and Yvonne turned to Blake, a wistful look in her eyes.

"Now you understand, do you not?"

"Yes, I understand, mademoiselle," he replied softly. "Again I offer you immunity before I turn the yacht and prisoners over. It is now an unpleasant duty, but it is my duty, and must be done."

"I thank you, but I cannot accept it, James Pearson," she added, turning to the president, who had sunk into a chair, crushed by the senorita's contempt, "I and my companions are now your prisoners, but watch us well," she said, in mocking tones, "for we will escape if we can!"

Blake left the Fleur-de-Lys with a strange tug at his heart-strings. The wayward mademoiselle, with her wistful eyes and fascinating manner, had made a deep mark on the unimpressionable Blake, and although he had brought to a successful conclusion one of the most dangerous cases in his experience, he felt no sense of triumph as he was pulled across to the Corsair.

Senor Mendoza had heard from the senorita the truth about Pearson. He had refused to go over and see his old partner, and was only anxious to get started for London, when he could begin steps to separate his interests from those of Pearson.

Pedro's joyful reception brightened Blake up a bit, but as the yachts parted company that night, one heading for London and the other east for South America with her freight of prisoners, he walked to the rail and gazed over the misty water. Once again he murmured, as he had done months before, "Poor little girl!"

• • • • •

Some weeks later the returned Blake, Tinker, and Pedro sat once more at breakfast in the cosy Baker Street rooms.

Blake was reading the morning paper, and Tinker looked up as the detective uttered a sharp exclamation.

"What is it, guv'nor?" he asked.

"Listen to this, Tinker," he replied. "I will read it to you. It is a cable message from Salvarita, and you will find it of interest:

" 'News is at hand of the return of President Pearson on board the yacht Fleur-de-Lys. With him he brought the missing two millions of bullion, and, most extraordinary of all, a whole cargo of prisoners. President Pearson was at once interviewed, and gave a vivid account of his capture, and ended by ascribing his release and the capture of his captors to the famous British detective Sexton Blake.

" 'The people gave the returned president a rousing welcome, and great excitement reigned as he was carried to the palace and installed in his old apartments. His cargo of prisoners have been kept aboard the yacht to await punishment.'"

"Gee, guv'nor, he got a great reception, didn't he?" remarked Tinker.

"Yes, my lad; but wait. There is more yet. This is a later message:

" 'Typical of the rapid changes in some South American republics is the following message received as we go to press.

" 'A climax has been reached in the affairs of Salvarita. Senor Mendoza has cabled from London his resignation from the Ambassadorship to England, and has also cabled a long denunciation of his former friend and partner, President Pearson.

" 'Senor Martina proceeded to the palace to inform the president. As he approached the council chamber he heard a shot, and a man rushed out with a smoking revolver in his hand. Senor Martina feared something serious had occurred, and endeavoured to seize the man, but failed.

" 'Calling to the guards to warn them, he hastened in to the council chamber, and found his worst fears realised. President Pearson lay on the floor already dead, adding another to the long list of the assassin's bullet. The guards succeeded in catching the assassin—one Gomez—who proved to be a soldier recently discharged in disgrace from the army. To complicate matters, the prisoners on the yacht Fleur-de-Lys, who were awaiting trial for the abduction of the late president, and the stealing of the now famous bullion, have overpowered their guards and recaptured the yacht.

" 'The guards were set adrift in the harbour in small boats, and the last seen of the yacht was the smoke from her funnel as she disappeared over the horizon.

" 'Our representative has interviewed Senor Mendoza, who confirms the above.' "

"Crikey, guv'nor," exclaimed Tinker, "things have certainly been moving in Salvarita, haven't they?"

"They certainly have," smiled Blake. "It looks as though I might again run up against the charming mademoiselle," he added to himself, "And it's a curious thing Fate has intervened and given her her revenge, as it did with Bechstein."

"Well, Tinker, let's to work," he continued aloud, rising; and they entered the consulting-room where so many exciting trails had their origin.

•   •   •   •   •

On a dreary, foggy night, not long after the events just related, a white yacht, looking ghostly in the creeping mist, stopped her engines and lay to off a lonely spot on the English coast.

The name Fleur-de-Lys was painted on her bows, and a slim, bronze-haired girl in a heavy coat stood on the bridge.

"This will do, captain," she said, turning to Captain Vaughan. "Have them lower the boat here,"

The captain turned to issue instructions, and a few moments later four sailors took their places in the boat.

"Bring up the prisoner!" commanded Yvonne.

Two more went below. They appeared shortly with a man in irons, and the man was Rymer,

"Knock off his irons and land him there," continued Yvonne.

Once released, Rymer turned and began to demand a reversal of her decision, but Yvonne's teeth came together with a snap.

"No; it is impossible! What I have said, I have said. You came here on the understanding that my word was to be law. You deliberately broke the rules, and attempted to murder the boy. You have thrown away wealth and success, but that is your own fault. Leave now, please."

Rymer, seeing further argument was useless, turned and descended the ladder.

Swiftly the boat set him ashore, and a few moments later the yacht turned and headed through the fog for the sunny South Sea island.

Yvonne went below early, but before undressing she gazed long and earnestly at a rough pencilled sketch on the wall.

It was a sketch of Sexton Blake, and had been made secretly by Yvonne when she was for three days his prisoner, and, strange to say, a happy one.

THE END.

[35200 WORDS]

The End.

MY CHUMS,—

If you have enjoyed this splendid Yvonne and Sexton Blake yarn, please give a non-reader chum a chance to enjoy it as well. Remember, that another Yvonne and Blake yarn appears in three weeks' time, entitled:

"On the Brink of Ruin."

Please mention this, and tell your chums.

THE SKIPPER.

U. J.—488

MY CHUMS,—

If you have enjoyed this splendid Yvonne and Sexton Blake yarn, please give a non-reader chum a chance to enjoy it as well. Remember, that another Yvonne and Blake yarn appears in three weeks' time, entitled:

"On the Brink of Ruin."

Please mention this, and tell your chums.

The "SKIPPER" Addresses his "CREWS"

NEXT WEEK'S SUPERB YARN; "THE CASE OF THE EMIGRANT SLAVES."
Write to THE SKIPPER,
"Union Jack" Library,
The Fleetway House, Farringdon Street,
London, E.C.

There is a fine story coming next week—one that will satisfy even the most critical reader. Carlac and Blake utilise their wonderful powers to the very utmost, and at last Sexton Blake places his enemy in prison.

I want all my chums to read next week's yarn, for I confidently assure them that it is a really good, sound story, that will appeal to all tastes for literature.

Please tell all your chums that Count Ivor Carlac is sent to prison by Sexton Blake next week, and ask them not to miss reading how it comes about.

REPLIES IN BRIEF.

[I am always pleased to help my chums with advice on any matter in which they experience a difficulty, and always do so through the post, if a stamp be enclosed for reply; but if not, they may look for a brief reply here. Chums in want of an immediate reply should always enclose a stamp, as the earliest possible moment they can expect to see a reply in this column is FOUR WEEKS after date of letter to me, and not always so soon as that.—The Skipper.]

Books on Whistling,

"Want to Know."—I am sorry to say that I have failed to find any book published that will give you information on whistling. Watch the manner in which your friends hold their lips, and endeavour to imitate them. It is very kind of you to say such nice things about the **Union Jack,** and I thank you sincerely.

A Boy who Wants to Join the Army.

B. B. F.—As you have three bad teeth as well as weak eyes, I am afraid you would not be received as a recruit in any branch of the Army. Both of your defects, I should think, from the number of cigarettes you tell me you smoke each week, are due to the smoking habit, and, as your sincere friend, I advise you to give it up without delay.

B.A. CANTAB, v. C. B. R.

The little argument between my chums, caused by the letters of B.A. Cantab, and C. B. R., is getting very interesting indeed.

I am taking careful note of all letters on the subject, and, later, will decide on the majority.

Meantime, below will be found a very interesting letter from a girl chum, to whom I extend my hearty thanks.

"Oxford Street, W.

"January 20th, *1913.*

"To the Skipper.

"Dear Sir,—Allow me, a girl reader, to write a word of appreciation of the **Union Jack.** I think you are right in saying it is a paper far all ages and sexes. I think by common consent the Plummer yarns are far the best.

"I note there is a difference of opinion as to whether he might be allowed to succeed now and again. I venture to say emphatically 'Yes.' I It will be so different from the stereotyped detective yarns, in which the detective always wins. You are getting hold of the better class of readers without in any way losing the support of the millions, because you are not afraid to take a new line and create something original.

"Note the variety of 'Raffles' from which I am sure you are not too proud to glean a hint. The reader can never guess how on earth the tales will end.

"You need not let Sexton Blake's reverses be at all frequent.

"I am looking forward to Yvonne. I am sure she will be worthy of woman's pluck and wit.— Yours truly,

"Miss C. H"

Here is another letter on the same subject from a chum signing himself "North Countryman." Certainly his argument is a sound one! Read it for yourself.

"Ward Street,
"Hendon-in-Sunderland.
"January 19th, 1913.

"Dear Mr. Skipper,—I had meant to write you before, and now take the opportunity to second an excellent suggestion in your recent numbers, namely, to allow Plummer to win once in a while. Please do! It is the only fault of the **Union Jack** that the interest is less because one knows that Sexton Blake cannot fail.

"I saw a gentleman wrote to suggest that this would encourage admiration of criminals. He writes from Wales, and I am sorry he has such a poor opinion of British boys as to think that a successful coup for Plummer will make them want to copy him.

"We are sportsmen in Sunderland, and lovers of football. Why do we go to see Sunderland play? Because of the glorious uncertainty. We want to win; but there is no sport if the other side have no chance beyond a draw at the best of times.—Yours sincerely,
"NORTH COUNTRYMAN."

BRIEF ACKNOWLEDGMENTS.

Hearty thanks to all the following chums for interesting letters:

A. B., Glasgow; W. H., Liverpool; G. T. R., Liverpool; J. C., Stockport; W. McC., Lisburn; Miss E. A., Old Charlton; A. P., Southampton; Miss M. R., Montreal; "Friend," Chatham; A. 0. A., Croydon; J. B. H.; W. F., Stratford; G. D., Bristol; B. W. E.; R. W., Chippenham; "A Chum," Newport; W. T. Alford; F. O.N., Cork, "A 4U.J. Reader," Cape Town; "Constant Reader"; E. C., Hastings; W. Λ. F., S.E.; R. J. P., E.; F. O. F., Lincoln; "8 L'pool Lads"; L.C., Poplar; W. R., Leyton; A, E.; "A New Reader," Barrow-in-F.; L. E. O., Cardiff; "Constant Reader"; J. P., Durham; P. E., Hayes; R. P., Brighton; A. W. H., Pallion; A, S. J., Port Elizabeth; W. T., Wallsend; C. S., Montreal.

Printed and published weekly by the Proprietors, at The Fleetway House, Farringdon Street, London, England. Subscription, 7s. per annum. Agents for Australia: Gordon & Gotch, Melbourne, Sydney, Adelaide, Brisbane; and Wellington, N.Z. - South Africa: The Central News Agency, Ltd., Cape Town and Johannesburg. Saturday, February 15th, 1913.

This magazine also contains a serial story, **Charlie Gordon's Schooldays**, but some of the story is not available so it has been omitted. /drf.